Also by G.F. MILLER

Glimpsed

NOT IF YOU

BREAK UP

with

ME FIRST

G.F. MILLER

ALADDIN
NEW YORK   LONDON   TORONTO   SYDNEY   NEW DELHI

ALADDIN

An imprint of Simon & Schuster Children's Publishing Division
1230 Avenue of the Americas, New York, New York 10020
First Aladdin paperback edition June 2024
Text copyright © 2024 by Simon & Schuster, LLC
Cover illustration copyright © 2024 by Jessica Cruickshank
Also available in an Aladdin hardcover edition.
All rights reserved, including the right of reproduction in whole or in part in any form.
ALADDIN and related logo are registered trademarks of Simon & Schuster, LLC.
Simon & Schuster: Celebrating 100 Years of Publishing in 2024
For information about special discounts for bulk purchases, please contact
Simon & Schuster Special Sales at 1-866-506-1949 or business@simonandschuster.com.
The Simon & Schuster Speakers Bureau can bring authors to your live event. For
more information or to book an event contact the Simon & Schuster Speakers Bureau
at 1-866-248-3049 or visit our website at www.simonspeakers.com.
Designed by Heather Palisi
The text of this book was set in Adobe Caslon Pro.
Manufactured in the United States of America 0424 MTN
2 4 6 8 10 9 7 5 3 1
Library of Congress Cataloging-in-Publication Data
Names: Miller, G.F., 1977– author.
Title: Not if you break up with me first / G.F. Miller.
Description: First Aladdin paperback edition. | New York : Aladdin, 2024. | Audience: Ages 10
and Up. | Summary: Best friends Eve and Andrew go to their first eight grade dance together,
and suddenly everybody assumes they are dating, so they each try and arrange a break-up—
except they are both beginning to feel a different kind of attraction.
Identifiers: LCCN 2023040899 (print) | LCCN 2023040900 (ebook) | ISBN 9781665950015
(hardcover) | ISBN 9781665950008 (paperback) | ISBN 9781665950022 (ebook)
Subjects: LCSH: Teenagers—Juvenile fiction. | Best friends—Juvenile fiction. | Dating (Social
customs)—Juvenile fiction. | Interpersonal relations—Juvenile fiction. | CYAC: Teenagers—
Fiction. | Best friends—Fiction. | Friendship—Fiction. | Dating—Fiction. | Interpersonal
relations—Fiction.
Classification: LCC PZ7.1.M5682 2024 (print) | LCC PZ7.1.M5682 (ebook) | DDC 813.6
[Fic]—dc23/eng/20240111
LC record available at https://lccn.loc.gov/2023040899
LC ebook record available at https://lccn.loc.gov/2023040900

To all the tenderhearted guys trying to figure it out. I see you.

Chapter 1
It's Only Weird If You Make It Weird

Eve was convinced that the clock in the airport terminal was set to Mercury time. Every minute took approximately fifty-eight times longer than a regular Earth minute.

"Didn't their plane land, like, an hour ago?" she demanded when she couldn't take it anymore.

"Fifteen minutes," her mom said, not looking up from her sudoku. "And I have no control over airline efficiency."

"Sorry," Eve muttered, dropping into a runner's lunge right there in front of the TSA and everybody. Running and prepping to run were Eve's go-to fixes for practically every problem—boredom, nervousness, awkward silences, cramps, loneliness, parents having their twentieth fight of the week. . . .

She glanced around the O'Hare International Airport waiting area, considering doing a couple of laps between the "Nuts on Clark" popcorn stand and the PASSENGERS ONLY BEYOND THIS POINT sign.

That would be weird, right? She should probably stick to stretching.

If people knew what she was going through, though, they wouldn't judge. Her best friend in the world had been gone for two whole months. (Because two-month family trips are a thing you can do when your dad's a teacher and your mom's job is virtual.) Two months was cruel. It was inhumane.

Eve had been forced to hang out with the other Cross Country girls all summer, which wasn't really a bad thing. They were pretty cool, and they *were* her teammates. But it meant she had a whole new friend group that Andrew wasn't part of. Plus they watched makeup tutorials and talked about which boys they liked. She wasn't being fake with them when she went along with it, but she wasn't totally being herself, either. With Andrew, she didn't have to pretend at all. She really missed that.

But now she was just a few Mercury minutes from seeing Andrew again.

It's bananas how much stuff can happen to a person in two months. Andrew turned fourteen and Eve wasn't there to smash cake in his face. Cross Country got a new coach.

The Gonzaleses moved away. Her friend Reese *kissed someone* on the *actual lips*. School started, and Andrew missed the whole first week of eighth grade. Eve's parents were acting horrible to each other, and she couldn't talk to her best friend about it.

And yeah, they'd been texting, kind of. But some things just aren't textable. Plus their mothers had colluded, as always, and put a million ridiculous restrictions on both of their phones. No phones at the dinner table. No phones in the car. No phones during "mandatory family time." Sometimes she'd wait hours for a text back, and finally get a **Sorry MFT** 😊. Worst of all, the things literally shut down at eight p.m. With Andrew on Florida time, all communication with her best friend was cut off before toddlers go to bed.

Thinking about everything she had suffered made Eve groan out loud. The lady in the TSA uniform standing guard under the PASSENGERS ONLY sign gave her a pointed look.

Eve switched legs, wailing, "I'm dying!"

"Of impatience?" Mom teased.

"Of old age!"

That got a *ha* from Mom.

Eve said, "Seriously, how long has it been?"

"Since your birth? Thirteen years and seven months. Since they landed?" Mom glanced at her watch. "Eighteen minutes."

How had only three minutes passed since the last time check? *See,* thought Eve, *Mercury time.*

Mom uncrossed her legs and recrossed them, opposite leg on top. Her sneaker-clad foot bounced, as she penciled a "5" into one of the boxes of her puzzle. The permanent crease between her eyebrows was deeper than usual. For all her calm façade, Eve could tell she was anxious too. Turned out even adults with unfettered phone access missed their besties. Eve put her forehead on her knee and focused on the sensations of stretching. The tightness of her calf and heel. The tension in her thigh.

"There they are!" Mom exclaimed, standing. "Is that *Andrew*?!"

Eve popped out of her lunge and scanned the crowd. Andrew was emerging from the security corridor. He was wearing running pants and a Miami Heat basketball jersey. He had a backpack slung on his shoulder, a rolling bag dragging behind him, and a shopping bag in the other hand. His mom, dad, and sixteen-year-old brother flanked him. Eve didn't take time to notice anything else. She took off running like she'd heard the starting gun at a Cross Country meet.

Andrew broke into a huge smile. He opened his arms and yelled, "McNugget!"

She fully left her feet when she crashed into him. He let

his bags fall as he caught her. Eve squealed, "I'm going to hug you so hard, you pass out!"

"I'm gonna crack your ribs," Andrew laughed back, his voice deeper than she remembered. But that didn't matter. All that mattered was that he was squeezing her *so* tight. And man, he must have gotten stronger. It really was hard to breathe.

"I'm going to break your spine," Eve wheezed, grabbing her own wrists and using the leverage to tighten her arms like a nutcracker. Her effort was rewarded with an *oof* from Andrew. She laughed victoriously with the little air she had left in her lungs.

Best. Hug. Ever.

Except Andrew was different. At least two whole inches taller than when she'd hugged him goodbye. Taller and stronger and deeper-talking. It was disorienting.

So much can happen in two months.

"Whenever you guys are done making out, we can go," Andrew's brother, Tom, huffed, hefting his backpack.

What?! Eve pushed away from Andrew almost as hard as she'd tackled him a minute ago. Andrew averted his eyes, his cheeks going red, and scratched his head like he always did when he was uncomfortable.

"Hey!" Mrs. Ozdemir cuffed Tom on the arm.

"Just kidding, jeez," Tom said.

It's just Tom being Tom, Eve told herself. But kidding or not, Tom's comment hung between them, making everything weird.

The moms turned back to their own reunion—jabbering and hugging like nothing had changed between them. Because nothing had.

Andrew cleared his throat and put on a forced-looking smile, seemingly determined to shake off whatever that was. He said, "Hey, I got you something!"

He retrieved the shopping bag he'd dropped and shoved it into Eve's hands. She reached in and unfurled a beach towel. It was a map of Florida—obnoxiously fluorescent green and blue, and peppered with cartoonish icons of mouse ears, palm trees, alligators, and creepy smiling oranges.

"It's so ugly!" Eve exclaimed, realizing that Andrew hadn't changed so much after all. He was still her goofy best friend. She smiled hugely. "My eyes are bleeding!"

Andrew grinned back, for real this time. "I figure this could help you suck less at geography."

"But if I was good at geography on top of everything else," Eve said, "that wouldn't really be fair to the other kids."

Andrew snort-laughed.

"Okay, guys, let's keep moving," Mr. Ozdemir prodded tiredly. The group started to move forward, quickly falling into their natural pattern—Mr. Ozdemir and Tom in the lead, the moms right behind, chattering and barely watching where they were going, and Eve and Andrew at the back of the line.

Eve held the beach towel on display behind her like winning runners do with flags at the Olympics, while Andrew told her about Florida. He talked about the Keys, the beach, a sailboat ride, petting alligators, and visiting a town hilariously named Sopchoppy.

"Your haircut looks kinda sopchoppy, no offense," Eve said.

"Did you sopchoppy your pants up on purpose?" Andrew countered.

They were both laughing as they dodged and weaved through baggage claim, keeping their moms in sight. But as they arrived at Carousel 4, where a crowd was already gathered to watch luggage trickle onto a conveyor belt, Andrew said, "How come your dad didn't come?"

Eve bit her lip. She wanted to tell Andrew everything that was going on, but she didn't know how to start, and this definitely didn't seem like the right time and place, with her mom right there and everything. Besides, Eve didn't know why her parents had started fighting—just that they were fighting. A lot. About everything. So she said, "It's complicated."

Andrew turned to look at her and leaned closer, his eyebrows pinched together. "Is it that bad?" he asked.

Before Eve could come up with an answer, she heard her mother say, "Look at them. They're so sweet together."

And Andrew's mom went, "Aaaaaaw."

What the actual heck?

Andrew must have heard it too, because they both stepped back at the same time, looking anywhere but at each other. Why did it have to be weird again?

Thankfully, the awkward moment was cut short by Mr. Ozdemir calling, "Andrew, red bag! Grab that one!"

Andrew reached for it. And that's when Eve realized that even more things had changed when she wasn't looking. Andrew kind of had *muscles*. Not like NBA muscles. But his arms were not the same skin-and-bones-with-pointy-elbows appendages he'd been jabbing her in the ribs with since kindergarten.

And, also, *armpit hair*.

From this moment on, Eve thought, *time will be measured before and after armpit hair.*

Before armpit hair, they were just *kids*. And even though there had been a razor in her shower for months, Eve had still thought of her and Andrew as kids. But now—hauling a red suitcase off a conveyor belt with his boy muscles and his hairy armpits—Andrew obviously wasn't a kid anymore. He was a *boy*. Like he always was, but now it mattered.

Not to Eve. It didn't matter at all to Eve, no matter what

awkward comments his brother and their moms made. She'd been best friends with Andrew forever. They'd seen each other through growth spurts, family drama, and broken bones. Their moms were practically conjoined. Their families did holidays together. Just because Andrew happened to be a boy—a tall, hairy boy—didn't mean anything had to change between them.

Eve clutched her new Florida beach towel. A cartoon alligator grinned up at her, and she whispered to it, "Don't worry, Alli G. Absolutely nothing is going to change."

Chapter 2
Not One Single Thing Doesn't Change

Starting school a week after everybody else wasn't supposed to be a big deal. Since Andrew's dad's district started later, his parents decided to stay in Florida until the last possible minute. When Andrew had protested, his dad had said, "Don't worry about it. The first few days, everybody's relearning how to be in school mode. And then it's all review for a couple weeks. You won't miss anything."

Wrong. He had missed a lot. Andrew felt like everyone else had a rhythm already, and he couldn't keep a beat. The teachers knew everyone's name except his—they kept calling him Andy, and he *hated* that. Everybody knew their locker combinations, their seat assignments, and which teachers were out for blood. Meanwhile, Andrew had spent his entire lunch period in the office because his lock didn't work and he was in the wrong math class.

All the guys had already told each other their summer stories and moved on. The girls had already formed posses and were roaming the halls like dangerous, unapproachable pack animals.

Last year, the guys had mainly talked about video games and LEGOs. Today they'd spent the whole time talking about which girls they liked.

He was even out of sync with Eve. Everything had seemed great when they were walking to school together, but the second they were inside the fence, one of her running friends had called to her, and she'd abandoned him. Later, when he saw her in the hall and tried to say hi, she didn't even look his way. He figured she must not have noticed him, so he tried to get her attention. But then the pack of girls she was with had given him weird looks and started whispering to each other, and Eve had gone bright red.

He hadn't heard a single thing the teacher said in social studies after that, because he spent the whole class trying to figure out why that was so gross and awkward and what he had done wrong.

It was a relief to get to band seventh period because at least the band room felt the same. Clarinets and flutes sat in the front two rows—mostly girls who assembled their instruments while they chatted or sucked on reeds. Behind them were saxophones, trumpets, trombones, and one tuba player. Everyone warmed up on scales or played random lines of music, creating a jumble of noise that made Andrew feel like he was home. In the very back, the percussion section added to the chaos by practicing rhythms on practice pads, snares, rims, their thighs, the wall. . . . Andrew headed toward them.

"OZZIE!" Mateo Ramirez shouted over the din.

"RAMIREZ!" Andrew held up his hand, and they high-fived.

"Where ya been?" Ramirez asked.

"FLORIDA," Andrew yelled back, snagging a pair of drumsticks and spinning one in his fingers.

"HEY, OZ! Welcome back, man," Jamal said. "You got here just in time."

"Yeah," Arav said, giving Andrew a fist bump. "We have to play for Handen today, and he's going to assign parts."

"Oh, okay." Andrew tried to play it cool, even though he was really ticked at his parents now. If he got stuck on bass drum—or worse, cymbals—for the whole marching season because he hadn't had time to practice, it would be all their fault.

Thankfully, the drumline played the same cadences and the school fight song every year. He had memorized the snare parts in seventh grade, but he was really hoping to play quads this year. Plus the band would have a new parade piece he'd need to learn. He asked, "What's the song this year?"

"'Uptown Funk,'" Jamal said, holding out the sheet music for snare drum.

"Do you have the quad part?" Andrew asked.

"She's got it," Ramirez said, pointing.

Andrew's gaze followed Ramirez's finger to a girl with short black-and-pink hair and heavy black eyeliner. She was pounding on four practice pads with mallets and ignoring them completely.

"Who is *that*?" She looked like she belonged in a rock band, and Andrew couldn't keep the awe out of his voice.

Ramirez and Jamal immediately started ribbing him with *oooooh*s and *aaaaaaaaw*s and kissing noises. Andrew wanted to climb inside the bass drum to get away from it. Thankfully, Arav jabbed him with a mallet and said, "Dude, it's Madison. Don't you recognize her?!"

"Madison Streeter?!"

"Yup."

Andrew had so many questions, but the guys were losing interest, going back to the rhythms and rudiments they'd been messing around with before he'd come in. He had no choice but to approach Madison if he wanted a peek at the quad part. And if he didn't get put on quads this year, he wouldn't be able to audition for the Blue Devils next summer. The Blue Devils were the best drum corps in the world, and Andrew had been dreaming about joining since fifth grade. He peeled away from the guys and went to stand by her, their hoots and sniggers barely audible amidst all the other noise in the room.

"HEY. MADISON?"

She looked up, continuing to tap out paradiddles. "OH. HI, ANDREW."

"You changed your hair." That was an understatement. Last year she'd worn it in a long brown braid every day. She'd also had glasses and braces.

"YEAH?" Her tone clearly made the word mean, *What do you want?*

"And you wear makeup now."

Madison made a face—lips pursed, eyebrows quirked—that said, *You'd better have a good reason to still be talking to me.*

Normally, Andrew would back away slowly now. But he focused on the Blue Devils and said, "Sorry, um, can I look at the quads music?"

Her face smoothed out, and she shrugged. "I'm using the fight song right now. You want 'Uptown Funk,' and we could trade in a couple minutes?"

Andrew gratefully accepted her offer and started studying

the music. Madison leaned in and said over the noise, "I guess you're my competition for quads, huh?"

"I guess." Andrew smiled at her, even though he was dead serious about getting picked to play the one and only set of quads. She smiled back with a clear "don't get your hopes up" vibe.

One of the trombone players leaned back and said, "ARE YOU GUYS DATING?"

"WHAT?"

"NO." Madison abruptly went back to pounding on her practice pads.

Why does this keep happening to me? Andrew thought. He shifted away from Madison and didn't look at her again for the rest of band.

Andrew and Madison both got picked for quads. Turned out the Band Boosters had bought a new set over the summer. But Mr. Handen chose Madison for drumline captain, and he warned Andrew to practice hard because he had a lot of catching up to do.

As soon as he got home from school, Andrew went to the backyard and practiced on four upturned buckets until it was getting too dark to read his music. He finally went in, his nose running from the cold, and the smell of dinner wafting from the kitchen. After he put his mallets and music into his backpack, he saw he'd missed three texts from Eve.

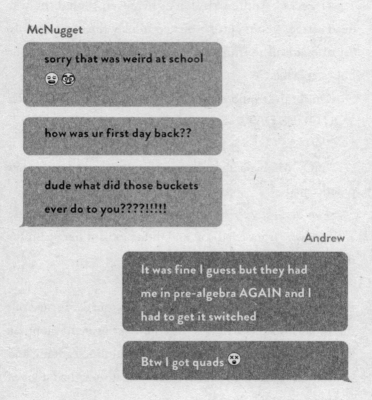

McNugget

sorry that was weird at school 😩 🤬

how was ur first day back??

dude what did those buckets ever do to you????!!!!!

Andrew

It was fine I guess but they had me in pre-algebra AGAIN and I had to get it switched

Btw I got quads 😵

"What are you grinning at, Snot Rag?" Tom asked, knocking into him with his shoulder.

"Ugh. I'm just texting Eve."

"Tell your *gurlfriend*—"

"She's not my girlfriend!" Andrew snapped.

"Sorry—you only wish."

"I do not!"

Tom had gone through several phases of teasing Andrew about Eve. He used to call her Andrew's twin sister. Then for a while he said Andrew was Eve's shadow. Or her puppy. Last year he would always make remarks about interrupting Eve and Andrew's "girl time" until their dad had made him stop. But the girlfriend joke was getting under Andrew's skin faster than anything else ever had.

Tom could obviously tell he'd hit a nerve, because he made a kissing noise and moaned, "Oooooh, Eve."

Andrew punched him in the shoulder. Tom put Andrew in a headlock and scrubbed his knuckles into his scalp. Andrew planted his feet and used his body weight to push Tom into the end table.

"What was that crash?!" Mom called from the kitchen. "Guys, come to dinner!"

Tom and Andrew took turns punching each other from the family room to the kitchen. When they sat down, they switched to kicking under the table.

"Cut it out, you two," Mom said, setting a casserole dish between their plates. She sat down, glanced at both of them, and said, "What are you fighting about?"

"Tom keeps riding me—"

"Andrew's being a drama queen about his crush."

"Shut up!" Andrew shouted.

Mom calmly scooped chicken-broccoli casserole onto their plates. "Who's the girl?"

"Eve, of course. Who else?" Tom shoveled the first steaming bite into his mouth and then sucked air like it was burning.

Mom sigh-smiled like she did during the end credits of her cheesy old eighties movies. Even though there were strands of gray in her dark hair, she looked all moony like the girls in those movies.

Andrew insisted, "I don't have a crush on her. We're just . . . We're—"

They were just best friends. Weren't they? He loved hanging out with her. She always made him laugh. Like friends do. But he'd missed her a lot this summer. And yesterday at the airport he had noticed she looked really pretty. And then he felt like crap when she ignored him today at school. Did that mean he liked her as more than friends? They'd always been friends. Why couldn't things stay simple?

"Whatever, dude. But you'd better start chewing gum or something, 'cuz no girl wants to kiss your Taki breath."

Andrew was sure Mom would yell at Tom, but she just chuckled into her casserole.

"Are you serious?" Andrew asked, wondering if he really

had bad breath. Maybe that's why Madison looked so much like she wanted him to stop talking to her in band.

"Yeah, dude, your breath reeks. Your pits, too."

"Do girls really notice stuff like that?" He looked at his mom for confirmation, fighting the urge to sniff his armpit.

"They notice," she said, "But you don't 'reek.' Brush your teeth. Shower. Wear deodorant."

"I *do*," Andrew protested.

"Then don't worry about it."

Too late. Andrew was already hard-core worrying about it.

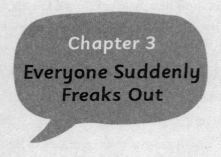

Chapter 3
Everyone Suddenly Freaks Out

Nina Moreno burst into the locker room looking like she'd already done the run for today. Her bronze cheeks were flushed dark red, and she seemed out of breath. Eve looked up from tying her running shoes. "Are you okay?"

Nina squeezed her eyes closed and ran in place for a second before announcing breathlessly, "I asked Brendan to the dance, and he said yes!"

The other Cross Country girls *squee*d and gasped and pressed her for details. Eve didn't want to be the only one not freaking out, so she jumped up with everyone else and tried to act jazzed, even though, until that moment, she'd assumed everyone would go to the dance in friend groups like they did last year.

Destiny Williams said, "No way! What did you say? What did he say?"

"I was like, 'Hey, want to go to the dance with me?' And he was like, 'Yeah, that'd be cool.'"

"Oh my gosh," Sofia cooed. "You are so, so brave. I really want Mark Chen to ask me, but I would *never* ask him first."

The whole team broke into a "you can do it . . . just go for it . . . there's no way he won't ask you" pep talk for Sofia. Eve did her best to add the right encouraging phrases and head bobs.

The chime signaling the start of after-school activities got them all moving toward the multisport field but did nothing to slow their conversation.

"Reese," Destiny said, "you're going with Jamal, right?"

"Yeah," Reese said with a sly smile. "I mean, he hasn't said anything about it yet, but yeah."

Eve knew Reese and Jamal had kissed under the bleachers on Friday, because Reese had told the whole team on the Cross Country group chat. No one had talked about anything else all weekend. And Destiny had described in vivid detail how she'd made out with a boy at camp over the summer. Now Nina and Brendan were a thing, and it seemed like Sofia and Mark would pair up any day.

Eve was *really* starting to get worried about being left behind. She didn't think she wanted to kiss anyone, but there was no way she was going to miss the first dance of eighth grade because she was the only one without a date.

"Eve, what about you?" Nina asked, coming alongside her.

"She's going with Andrew, of course!" Destiny said.

Of course?! Eve tried not to look surprised or confused. She was friends with Andrew. But why did everyone assume they would go together? She tried to sound sure of herself when she said, "Um, I mean, maybe. But we're just friends."

Reese snorted. "Yeah right."

Destiny had pulled ahead. She turned to face them, walking backward with total confidence. "Maybe when we were kids. But *now?* The way he was *looking* at you yesterday?"

Sofia sighed dreamily. "It was sooooo sweet."

"That's just how he looks," Eve said, sounding less confident than she'd meant to. The truth was, it had been different—that look. Or maybe she was imagining it.

Andrew had only been back two days, and there had already been so many awkward moments, first at the airport and then at school yesterday. When he'd called to her and tried to wave her over, all the girls had started arguing about whether their ship name should be "Andreve" or "Evedrew." She felt bad about ignoring him, but what else could she do? If she'd gone and talked to him, everyone would have said he was her boyfriend.

None of this had been a problem Before Armpit Hair.

They were just friends, and no one made a big deal about it. Armpit hair ruined everything.

"But if he asked you, you'd say yes, right?" Sofia pressed.

Eve felt her face get hot. She mumbled, "Um, yeah, maybe."

The group reached the track and started stretching.

"Actually, I heard Andrew and Madison might be a thing," Nina said, standing on one leg and holding her foot behind her butt.

"Oh yeah, I heard that too," Reese said from a deep lunge. "I guess they were flirting in band pretty hard-core."

Wait. *WHAT?!* There were about a hundred and twenty problems with that. First, her best friend was not allowed to go off and like someone without *telling her about it*. She shouldn't have to find out things about him from the Cross Country team. What was happening to their friendship?! Second, if Andrew started dating someone, Eve really would be the last person still acting like a little kid while everyone else on the freaking planet had leveled up. Third, if Andrew dated Madison, how would he still hang out with Eve? Was he dumping her as a friend? Had he . . . outgrown her?

Her face must have given away her anxiety, because Reese said, "Oh my gosh, you didn't know?"

"Are you okay?" Sofia asked, real concern in her voice.

"Don't worry, he definitely likes *you*," Destiny said, trying to reassure her.

"You should ask him quick before she does, though," Nina said—obviously wise and emboldened from her recent victory with Brendan.

Her advice ignited an impassioned pep talk from the rest of the team: "Yes!" "Go for it!" "Do it, girl." "Ask him NOW! He's right over there!"

Eve looked to the center of the field, where the drumline was warming up. Andrew was wearing four drums on a harness—the "quads" he'd been obsessing over since last year. Madison was standing next to him in the same rig, but they didn't seem to be flirting at the moment. Jamal, Arav, and a few other people were carrying snare drums, bass drums, cymbals. . . . She really didn't want to go over and talk to him in front of all these people. She wanted it to be just the two of them, when everything felt easy.

"Oh my gosh," Sofia said, "He looks so, *so* cool with his drums. And, I mean, he's *soooo* good. No wonder so many girls like him."

Eve had never thought of Andrew's drums as cool. There had been way too many hours of hearing him practicing in his backyard for this particular Andrewism to hold any mystique. Drumming was just a thing he did . . . sometimes too much. When did he get "*soooo* good"? When did "so many girls" start liking him? He was *hers*, dang it. Her best friend. Who were these girls?

"Yeah, and he's super cute," Destiny added. The team agreed with hums and giggles.

They weren't wrong—Andrew *was* cute. He had thick, dark hair and brown eyes that crinkled into half-moons when he laughed. He had dimples and clear skin, and he'd grown at least two inches and gotten muscles and armpit hair and oh no, *oh no*, oh NO. Madison probably *did* like Andrew. With her spiky pink hair and her eyeliner and her drum kit, Madison was a thousand times cooler than Eve. Of course he would like her back. Eve was suddenly sure she was about to be left out and left behind.

Destiny gave her an encouraging shove in Andrew's direction. "You got this!"

"Just ask him," Nina commanded.

Eve took a step and then another, kind of wishing for her own personal black hole to disappear into.

"Woo! Get it!" Reese said, and the whole team cheered.

Andrew must have heard them because he looked over and locked on Eve. No going back now.

Eve took a bracing breath and marched toward the drumline, who were now *all* watching her approach. She just had to get this over with, like a geography test.

No more thinking, she told herself, *only doing.*

When she was inside Andrew's six-foot space bubble, she blurted, "Wannagotothedancewithme?"

"Uhhhhh." Andrew's face turned five shades of red. He was chewing gum (which Eve could hardly ever remember him doing), but stopped midchew, mouth open. His drumsticks stilled too. The whole drumline had gone silent and was staring at them. It was worse than Mercury time—time had frozen altogether. Eve's legs itched to run, to get far away from this quagmire of awkwardness. Andrew swallowed, his Adam's apple visibly bobbing, before finally saying, "Sure."

"Cool," Eve said. Then she turned and ran.

Chapter 4
Nothing Makes Sense Anymore

Andrew was sure of one thing. He had swallowed his gum. He watched—burning with embarrassment—as Eve ran away. She hadn't gone more than five steps when the drumline's moment of silence broke into a cacophony of hoots, kissing noises, and rim shots. Madison burst out laughing. Andrew could feel sweat beading on the back of his neck and worried that he wasn't wearing enough deodorant.

"DUDE!" Jamal jabbed him in the ribs with his drumstick.

"Naw-iiiiiice-aaaah." Ramirez managed to turn the word "nice" into three long syllables.

Holden, the first-chair trumpet player, appeared in their midst. "Did Eve seriously just ask you out?"

It seemed like a simple enough question, but Andrew choked on the answer. She must have asked him as a friend, which obviously didn't count as "asking him out." But then why did she make a big scene in front of the whole band when she could have just texted him or talked to him after school or something? Did that mean she actually *liked* him? Andrew didn't understand anything anymore. So he said, "Uhhhh—"

"Yeah, she asked him to the dance," Arav filled in helpfully.

"Daaawg!" Holden punched Andrew in the back. "She got *hot*." He waggled his eyebrows at the guys and did a chin bob in Madison's direction. She glared at him, smacking her mallets against her palm threateningly. Holden laughed and walked away, playing the riff from "Uptown Funk."

Something about Holden rubbed Andrew the wrong way. No. Scratch that. *Everything* about Holden rubbed Andrew the wrong way. His trendy hair, the little dice-throw move he did all the time to look cool, the ego trip he'd been on ever since he'd gotten first-chair trumpet, and *especially* the way he talked about girls. Hearing Holden say Eve "got hot" churned up some testosterone-driven caveman reaction in Andrew that caught him off guard. He imagined himself shoving Holden's face into the dirt and then instantly felt like a jerk.

Embarrassment, confusion, anger, and now guilt . . .

there were too many feelings all at once. Andrew was over-whelmed.

It was a relief when Mr. Handen called the band to attention and immediately counted off the school fight song. Andrew took all his problems out on his drums.

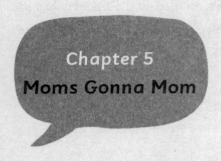

Chapter 5
Moms Gonna Mom

As she biked home after Cross Country practice, Eve put her mental armor on. She never knew what trauma she'd be dealing with at her house—tears, shouting, tense silence, muttered sarcasm—so she had to be ready for anything.

It wasn't even like they fought about important stuff. It was usually something nitpicky. Mom didn't like Dad's new car. Dad was annoyed that Mom rearranged the dishwasher after he loaded it. Mom didn't want to have to ask Dad to take the trash out—he should just do it—and Dad said he couldn't read minds. Stuff like that.

Sometimes Eve pleaded with them to stop fighting or attempted to distract them any way she could. Other times she pretended not to notice them glaring at each other. But mostly she just hid in her room with her earbuds in.

When she got to the house, Eve parked her bike in the garage, took a deep breath, and opened the door. She could hear her parents in the family room—they hadn't leveled up to screaming and throwing things, but their voices were sharp and angry.

"—you expect, Joanna?"

"Right. God forbid there be any *expectations* of you, David. I am so tired of giving a hundred and fifty percent. I'm tired of trying to explain why this isn't working."

"You think you're the only one who's *tired*? I'm tired of getting ambushed every time I walk in the door. I'm *tired* of—"

Eve put her head down and made a break for the stairs.

"Eve. You're home." Her mother's voice had fake calm layered over tension. With a sigh, Eve paused and waved. Her dad scrubbed his hand over his reddish beard and through his dark blond hair. Her mom was still dressed in scrubs from her job at the doctor's office, with her brown hair in a messy bun. She didn't smile as she asked the obligatory "How was your day?"

"Fine."

Her dad mumbled something about getting water. Her mom rolled her eyes as he escaped to the kitchen. Eve dug for her earbuds, muttering, "I'm gonna go get started on my homework."

Her mom's phone chirped an incoming text from Mrs. Ozdemir (there was a special tone just for her). Eve shifted her weight, wondering if she should run for it.

It only took a second for Mom to read her message. Her eyebrows went up, and she looked at Eve. A smile slowly spread across her face. Not a "put on a brave face for the kid" smile. A real one. A "this is exactly what I wanted for Christmas" smile. Eve couldn't remember the last time she'd seen it. Her mom said, "SO?!"

"So what?" Eve asked, because she really had no idea. Her stomach growled. Her feet hurt. There was a blister on her left heel. And she could smell herself—post-run BO. Gross.

"Sooooo," Mom sang. "You asked out Andrew?!"

"Oh. You. Um. What?"

"Do I get to hear about it?"

"It seems like Mrs. Ozdemir already told you."

Eve really *didn't* want to talk about it. The Cross Country girls had been freaking out about it during the whole three-mile run. She was already tired of talking about the stinking dance. What Eve really wanted was a change of subject, a hot shower, and just a huge amount of carbs. "Can we have spaghetti for dinner?"

Mom deflated a little. "Why won't you talk to me? This is a big deal!"

Eve was about to tell her mom that she and Andrew were only friends, and it seemed like the thing to do at the time, but it was ninety percent awkward, and she kind of wished she had never asked him. But something about Mom's eagerness triggered a memory.

It was Easter, seven or eight years BAH (Before Armpit Hair). She and Andrew had been dressed up in their Easter clothes, and their moms had been taking pictures like it was their actual job. Andrew had tugged at his bow tie while Eve spun circles to make her dress pouf out. She'd gotten so dizzy she'd fallen over and then started crying because her "boot-iful" dress had a big dirt stain. To make her feel better, Tiny Andrew had taken a striped plastic egg out of his basket and given it to her. It'd had a blue ring pop inside. He'd sat next to her in the dirt, and they'd taken turns licking the ring pop. And then she remembered Andrew's mom saying, "That counts, right? They're officially engaged now?" And Eve's mom had giggled and said, "These pictures are going side by side with their wedding photos. I can't even. They're so cute."

When Eve was five or whatever, she'd barely known what they were talking about. All she'd really cared about was the candy. But now, standing in her family room smell-ing like teen spirit, Eve realized that she was living some kind of secret arranged marriage conspiracy. Their moms had been hoping for this hookup their whole lives.

Eve froze. Her brain's reaction to this next-level weirdness was to perform a complete system reboot.

"Eve, are you okay, honey? You look like you're in shock."

Before the higher-level brain functions came back online, Eve's instincts kicked in. She grabbed one foot behind her butt—focusing on balancing on the other foot and the stretch in the front of her thigh. "Yeah, I'm . . . I'm just . . . uh . . ."

Dad returned, buying Eve some time. He gave Eve a side hug and said, "Sorry about that. Welcome home, Road Runner."

Mom said, "Eve, tell Dad your *news*."

Dad perked up. "News? What's going on, Evie?"

It wasn't direct address, but it was *almost* like they were talking. Like the topic of Andrew was somehow—at least for this moment—a bridge back to how things used to be. Eve switched legs. She let her voice pitch higher like Nina's had when she was freaking out about Brendan. "I asked Andrew to the fall formal!"

The Nina impression worked like magic. Mom giddy-clapped, and Dad's eyes got big. Then, like a miracle, Mom *looked at Dad* and said, "Our little girl is growing up."

She turned to Eve. "You'll need a dress. And shoes."

Dad blew out a dramatic breath. "Oh man, how much is this going to set me back?"

And they laughed. Both of them. *Laughed.*

Eve still had no idea how everything had changed around her overnight, or why every girl she knew was suddenly acting like a Disney princess hopped up on Rockstar. She couldn't even begin to think about what all this meant for her and Andrew. But if her being excited about a dance would give her parents something to be on the same page about, then she was going to be peppier than the whole Disneyland Parade.

She jitter-stepped in place. "When can we go shopping???!!!"

Chapter 6
For One Moment, It's All Good

McNugget

so we're meeting at 5 tmrw for pics okay??!!!!!

Andrew

why so early?

McNugget

it's the golden hour I guess 🙆

so we'll look extra pretty 😂 😘

Andrew scratched his head, trying to decide how to respond. It had been two weeks of this—Eve over-enthusiastically texting about all things dance related. First it had been about how his shirt and tie should "coordinate" with her dress. Two days later his mom had assaulted him with lavender button-downs. Then it was "Let's wear matching Chucks!" Followed by his mom dragging him to the mall to find purple All Stars.

Then, a couple of days ago, Eve started texting about taking pictures. When he'd asked his mom why they had to do that, she'd said, "It's your first date. Don't you want to remember it?"

He'd said it wasn't really a date. And then she'd said, "I've already spent over a hundred dollars on clothes and shoes. It's a date."

Then he'd said he didn't need a photo shoot to remember the "date," and she'd said, "Well, Jo and I do."

Jo was Eve's mom's name. Andrew felt weirdly like his mom and Eve's mom and Eve were in on a secret. And they had conspired to make sure he never found out the secret. And the secret was about him.

"OZZIE!" Arav was gesturing to him to get in parade formation. The rest of the drumline was already lined up. Andrew stashed the phone and hefted his quad harness onto his shoulders.

"Ever since Oz got a girlfriend, he's always the last one ready," Jamal joked from the snare line as Andrew took his spot next to Madison.

"Well, ever since you *lost* your girlfriend, you also lost the *beat*," Ramirez shot back.

"Dude, I'm still better than you. Plus *I* broke up with *her*."

"You're all noobs," Madison muttered, just loud enough to be heard over the random drumrolls, honks, and blats of the band warming up.

Then Mr. Handen raised his arms, and everybody came to attention. He called, "Madison, warm up the drumline. Everybody else, C-scale."

Madison counted them off and they started rudiments. While he played *right, left, right, right, left, left,* he had plenty of time to think, *DO I have a girlfriend?*

He and Eve had never talked about dating. Everyone had just started referring to her as his girlfriend. At first he blew it off, but then she'd been texting him *so much* since she asked him to the dance. Not the normal, easy texts he was used to. Gushy texts with kissy emojis and too many exclamation points.

Did Eve like him?

Eve was amazing, so her maybe liking him was amazing. Or at least it *should* be amazing.

Except she still avoided him at school like he had a zombie virus. And they barely hung out anymore. The truth was, he really missed her. How was it possible to miss your maybe girlfriend who lived across the street, went to the same school, and texted you twenty times a day? Why did it feel like he was losing his best friend?

Andrew's thoughts continued to circle the Eve dilemma while the band practiced marching up and down the track, while they played the school fight song, while they rehearsed "Uptown Funk" twenty times in a row, and when Mr. Handen told them to go home and report in uniform tomorrow at eleven a.m. "And remember," he barked, "early is on time—"

"And on time is late!" Andrew shouted back along with the rest of the band.

Eve's strange behavior was on his mind as he said, "See you tomorrow," to the guys. It was on his mind during dinner and while he played *Super Smash Bros.* with Tom. And the next day while he got into uniform and marched in the parade. He was still trying to figure it out Saturday afternoon while he took a shower, gelled his hair into the coolest *shwoop* he could manage, put on his extremely lavender shirt, applied triple layers of deodorant, and retied his purple tie five times.

"Andrew! Ten minutes!" Mom called.

Tom pushed through the door and flopped onto Andrew's bed. "Nice pink shirt, dork."

"It's *lavender*."

"*You're* lavender."

"What does that even—" Andrew gave up without finishing the sentence. He surveyed his brother's T-shirt and basketball shorts. "Aren't you taking Brylie to the high school dance?"

"Nah. We're over each other. I'm going with Kenna."

"Well, don't you have to get ready?"

"Yeah, in like two hours."

"How come *you* don't have to take 'golden hour' photos?" Andrew complained.

Tom shrugged.

Andrew chewed his lip. "Can I ask you something?"

Tom grunted.

"Have you ever had a girl act, like, really into you on text but ignore you in person?"

Tom laughed. "Yeah, classic girl move."

"*Why?*"

Tom shrugged again. "Who knows? They're just weird like that." He adjusted the pillows behind his head. "You wanna use my Lucky cologne? Guaranteed to make girls flock to you."

"I don't really want a whole *flock*," Andrew admitted. Tom laughed again.

♥ ♥ ♥

They were supposed to meet Eve and Mrs. McNeil at the park by their house—the one they'd been playing at together since they were five. They used to sit in a wagon together, and their moms would pull them there. It felt kind of silly to drive three blocks, but Andrew figured it was illegal to walk in fancy clothes or something.

Andrew and his mom got there first, and while they waited, he sat in the swing, dragging his purple Chucks through the rubber chips and wondering what was going on with him and Eve. She'd been avoiding him so hard that he had no idea what to expect tonight. Between that and the tight-collared shirt, Andrew couldn't help but feel nervous.

He looked up when he heard a car door slam. Eve stood twenty or so yards away, just looking at him. The dress she had on showed curves he hadn't even known existed under her baggy T-shirts. Her hair was out of its typical ponytail and hung, shiny and wavy, past her shoulders. She looked so pretty that Andrew forgot to breathe.

Then she smiled, her nose crinkling up, and he forgot *everything*.

She sprinted toward him because Eve never walked if she could run. Coming to a stop right in front of his swing, she grinned down at him and said, "Wow! You clean up!"

Andrew was flustered. She was acting like her old self, finally. But she didn't look like her old self. At all. He wanted to ask her what the heck was going on, tell her she was beautiful, and crack a joke. All at the same time. But most of all, he didn't want to say something awkward and sound like a noob. He swallowed and said, "You too."

"Are you wearing cologne?!"

"Uhhhh."

He heard his mom's phone camera click. He cleared his throat. "I brought you something."

He held out the small box his mom had foisted on him.

Eve looked at it. "A corsage?" she guessed. Then she opened the lid and discovered a brownie. They both agreed that Andrew's mom made the best fudgy brownies in the known universe. Eve gasped. "This is SO much better! I love it!" Then she stuffed half of it into her mouth.

Andrew hoisted himself out of the swing so he was toe to toe with Eve. She was shorter than him. He'd noticed it at the airport, but he still wasn't used to it.

There was another camera click, and he saw Mrs. McNeil taking photos with Eve's dad standing next to her. Andrew thought her dad being here was maybe a good sign. Except Mr. McNeil looked a *lot* less excited than their moms did. Andrew wanted to ask about her parents and how she was feeling about things at home. But they couldn't talk about it now, not at this awkward photo shoot with their parents watching and listening to every word. He suddenly wished it was just him and Eve.

Eve polished off the brownie and one-shotted the box into the closest trash can. He was impressed, like always. When she turned back to him, her eyes twinkled in the golden light of the sunset. "Uh" was still the best he could do.

Without warning, she punched him in the chest. "You're it," she said. And then she was gone.

With a relieved laugh, Andrew took off after her. She dodged around playground equipment, turning around every few seconds to let him catch up, and then springing away just before he could tag her. Not that he was trying his hardest. He certainly wasn't going to tackle her into the rubber chips in her fancy dress. He still remembered how much she'd cried when she fell in the dirt in her Easter dress when they were little.

When Eve tried to run up the slide, Andrew saw his chance. He grabbed her by the ankle and yanked her back down. She screamed and then laughed as she crashed into his legs, almost knocking him over.

"No tag backs," he panted.

Eve untangled herself and stood, sweeping her hair back from her face. She was flushed and smiling . . . and looking right at him for the first time in weeks. Running maybe wasn't the only reason he was out of breath.

Click, click, click. "Get a little closer together," Mrs. McNeil instructed. "Look over here."

Andrew turned obediently toward the parental paparazzi and felt Eve's arms come around his shoulders from behind. She put her face right next to his, standing on the end of the slide to gain the height advantage.

Playing and laughing and hugging . . . it was everything he'd been missing about their friendship, plus something brand-new. This awareness that Eve was a *girl.* A really pretty girl. His heart felt like it was swelling too big for his chest cavity.

"Now look at each other," his mom commanded.

Obediently, Andrew turned his head to a drum fill of camera clicks. Eve turned too, so the tip of her nose was only inches from his. She was so close, he could practically taste the brownie she just ate. He felt his face getting hot, and his tie was choking him.

"Your breath's not as bad as usual," Eve said, her eyes twinkling again.

"Well, I brushed my teeth," Andrew bragged, like he'd invented it.

Eve cracked up, which felt amazing. Making Eve laugh was like getting the invincible star in *Super Mario Bros.*

Then Eve crossed her eyes and puffed out her cheeks,

and *he* cracked up—big gulping-air laughter that cleared his head and broke the weird tension between them. Eve watched him lose it and laughed again. Their parents took a barrage of photos before bustling them into his mom's car.

As their seat belts clicked, Andrew thought again about asking Eve why she'd been acting so weird lately. But he didn't want to bring it up with his mom in the front seat. Actually, maybe the bigger reason he couldn't say the words was because, for this moment, everything was good again. Why ask questions that might mess it up?

While he was trying to figure out what to do, Eve leaned over and punched him in the arm. "Punch buggy," she announced, pointing to a yellow VW Bug as it passed.

They played punch buggy the whole car ride, just like they always had since they were kids. Andrew wished it could be easy like this forever. But, as it turned out, it didn't even stay easy until they got inside the gym.

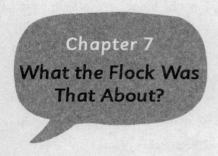

Chapter 7
What the Flock Was That About?

When they arrived at school, Andrew's mom shot him a look in the rearview mirror. Before Eve had a chance to wonder what it meant, he jumped out of the car, ran around, and opened the door on Eve's side. Eve hadn't made it all the way out of the car when the Cross Country group chat started blowing up her phone.

Sweet Sofia

OMG YOU GUYS ARE
ADORBS!!!!!

Destin-ation

Have you kissed him yet???

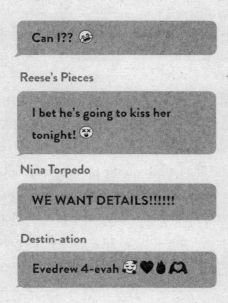

Can I?? 👻

Reese's Pieces

I bet he's going to kiss her tonight! 😵

Nina Torpedo

WE WANT DETAILS!!!!!!

Destin-ation

Evedrew 4-evah 😋 🖤 💧 👭

She fumbled the phone, desperately hoping Andrew hadn't seen any of those cringey texts. But then she realized he was busy fielding gestures and shouts from a group of drumline guys clumped near the gym door. She averted her eyes and spotted Reese and Destiny. They waved their phones in the air enthusiastically.

Meanwhile, his mom called out the driver's-side window, "Have fun! Mrs. McNeil will pick you up at nine."

"'Kay, Mom."

"You can always text."

"'Kay."

"Be a gentleman! Open doors."

"O-*kay*," Andrew said. Eve could see his cheeks turning maroon, even in the dim light.

"I love you both!"

Eve took pity on him and intervened. "Thanks for the ride, Mrs. O. See you later!" She grabbed Andrew's arm and pulled him toward the gym.

He smiled at her—like he had on the first day of school this year. His "something is different" smile. She hadn't minded him smiling like that when it was just them and their parents at the park. In fact, the smile was a good thing—sure to make her mom swoon with joy. And they'd had so much fun that it was easy to pretend they were back to normal and that she was just imagining him looking at her weird.

But now he was doing it again, with everyone staring at them and shipping them and thinking gross stuff about them that wasn't true at all. "Stop," she whispered.

"Stop what?"

"Don't look at me like that."

"Like *what*?"

"Just don't look at me!" she hissed. As they approached his rowdy friends, she dropped his arm and marched past without giving them a reason to tease her. Andrew lagged behind for a second before diving in front of her and pulling the gym door open as she was reaching for it. One of the guys behind them went, "Ooooooh."

Eve was mortified. "I don't need your big, strong boy muscles, *thanks*. I am capable of opening doors."

"I—I know," Andrew stammered, "but my mom—"

"Our moms aren't here. So just be normal, okay?"

Andrew's face was too easy to read. He didn't even try to hide his confusion, hurt, and embarrassment. Eve felt like a jerk. She wanted to give him a rib-crushing hug and a heartfelt apology, but with everyone looking at them, that was completely impossible. All she managed was a mumbled, "Sorry."

"Tickets?"

Eve and Andrew both turned. Ms. Lim, the math teacher, sat at a table with a money box. She repeated, "Do you have tickets?"

"Oh!" Andrew produced them, slightly crumpled, from his back pocket, and handed them to Ms. Lim. With a tilt of his head, he led the way into the dance.

Movies had gotten Eve's hopes way too far up about school dances. The decorations were about fifteen percent of what Hollywood had led her to believe. There were a few balloons and streamers. Some people posed for photos in front of a neon purple-and-green backdrop.

A middle-aged DJ with a laptop and two huge speakers blasted KIDZ BOP defiling a Taylor Swift song. There was a refreshments table with two-liter bottles of soda, bags of Takis, and Chips Ahoy!

Why did we get all dressed up for this? thought Eve. Maybe it was just her, but Takis and Coke seemed like they went best with jeans and hoodies.

"I see vee have zee finest hors d'oeuvres at our leetle soirée," Andrew said in a fancy chef accent.

Eve cracked up. Through her laughter, she said, "I *was* kind of picturing a chocolate fountain or something."

"I might have a melted candy bar in my pocket," Andrew said.

"Close enough!" Eve held her hand out expectantly.

"Oh, sorry, it's not for *you*. This is awkward."

"Give me that chocolate!" Eve growled.

"Death first!"

With mock rage, Eve executed a slo-mo karate punch. Andrew played along, reeling back before blocking her next strike. She aimed a kick at his legs, and he dramatically crumpled to the floor, clutching his knee. Even his cry of pretend pain was low, slow comedy gold. Eve could feel all the anxiety draining out of her. *This* was why Andrew was her best friend. He could always untangle her emotional knots with his comic timing and his spontaneous fight choreography. When she was a brat, he would always forgive her without making her explain.

Andrew swung at her in Mercury time from his position on the floor—a wide right hook. *This is good. We can do this,*

Eve thought as she blocked the punch. She could let go of all the pressure from her family and the girls, and they could just be Andrew and Eve like before. She smiled as she drove her fist toward his face. He went, "Nooooooo," and then rolled left just in time to dodge it.

"Dude, are you getting whooped on by a girl?" a guy named Mateo Ramirez said, as half the drumline descended on them.

Andrew popped up, brushing himself off. "Hey, guys."

"OZ! Up top!" Jamal called. They high-fived.

Except for Andrew, Eve tried to ignore boys, especially when they were clumped together. They were usually gross, immature, and making a lot of random noises. But curiosity got the best of her, and she blurted, "Jamal, didn't you come to the dance with Reese?"

"Nah. We broke up yesterday."

"What?! Why?" She wanted to stop talking, but words kept coming out of her mouth.

"She was just being annoying and stuff," Jamal said. "She would text me, and if I didn't text back in like five seconds, she'd be all mad."

"That's the worst!" Mateo agreed. "Or when they want to know what you're doing every minute. Like, girl, chill."

"I think it's weird when girls take guys' hoodies. What's that about?" Arav chimed in.

Eve was about to say *Hi! Girl here!* But just as she opened her mouth, a guy named Huston or Hudson swaggered up.

"Hey, homes!" He pantomimed throwing dice toward her feet. "Hey, guuurl."

Somehow, the way he said it, she could tell it was spelled with a *u*. She narrowed her eyes at him.

"Hey, Holden," the guys called back without much enthusiasm.

That's it, Eve thought, *Holden*.

Andrew shifted so he was standing right next to her. She shot him a nonverbal *what's up*. But he didn't notice. He was looking at Holden, who was looking at her all smirky. Eve had never been "checked out" before, that she was aware of, but she felt like maybe that was what was happening.

Holden jutted his chin toward her. "Eve, right? You look *smoking hot* tonight."

"Thank you?" She really didn't know if that was the right response.

Arav and Mateo both looked from Holden to Andrew and back again. Jamal had one eye squinted. Holden's eyebrows were going up and down. It was a silent conversation that was clearly *about* her but didn't include her. Eve couldn't resist glancing at Andrew for a clue to what was going on. She could always read his face.

What she saw set off alarm bells. It was his "I'm playing

along but I'm about to lose it on you" face—just one dimple popped and kind of a half-hearted chuckle that didn't make it to his eyes. She'd seen it plenty of times when his brother, Tom, was pushing his buttons on purpose. It usually preceded some furniture getting knocked over and their mom telling them to "take this big energy outside."

She had no idea what was going on with Andrew and Holden, but she felt a sudden need to break the tension. Otherwise, this night might include real-time punches and explaining to their parents how they ended up suspended from school. She darted a look toward the refreshments table. Maybe she'd make it rain Takis. That should lighten the mood.

Instead, Mateo escalated things. "Dude," he said to Holden. "Not cool."

"What?" Holden continued to smirk in her direction.

Suddenly Andrew's hand was engulfing hers. She was so surprised, she tried to jerk away. But instead of letting go, he tightened his grip, threading his fingers through hers possessively. Holden's smirk faded a little.

Jamal nodded toward the hand-holding. "Guy. Stop checking out Ozzie's girlfriend."

Bam. Mercury time. The word sounded like *g i i i i i r l - f r i e n n n n d.*

She wasn't anyone's girlfriend. There'd been a mistake.

"Yeah," Andrew confirmed, his voice cracking, his grip tightening.

Eve wanted to yell, *Wait! Stop!* But she couldn't make a sound.

Her brain was rebooting again—a blue screen of death with a giant flashing *ERROR: UNEXPECTED OPERATION.* Her hand was held hostage, and she couldn't move, couldn't think.

Jamal had said *girlfriend.*

And Andrew didn't correct him.

When had she become Andrew's girlfriend?!

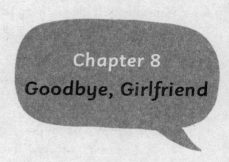

Chapter 8
Goodbye, Girlfriend

"Hey. We're cool," Holden said, showing his hands. "I'm just playin'."

Andrew was usually cool with everybody. He hated how easily Holden got under his skin. Right now, he really wanted to throw Holden to the ground *Super Smash Bros.* style.

When Eve grunted, he realized he'd been pouring all his irritation into squeezing her hand. "Sorry," he mumbled. She probably couldn't hear him over the Ramones song that had just come on. The moment he loosened his grip, Eve pulled away and put both hands behind her back. She stared hard at a spot outside their circle, and one of her purple Chucks jittered against the gym floor. Andrew knew she was ready to run, he just didn't know why.

"Well, see ya, losers," Holden said. "Ima go try to get Reese and Destiny to help me start a mosh pit."

The group watched him walk away, Jamal muttering something about Holden moving in on his girl.

"Um, I'm gonna . . . gotothebathroom," Eve announced, pulling Andrew's attention away from Holden's phony swagger-step. She took two backward steps, pivoted, and bolted for the double doors.

Called it, Andrew thought.

"Wow, she's *really* gotta go," Ramirez said, making Jamal and Arav cackle. Jamal produced an impressively realistic fire hose sound. From there, it became a competition to see who could get the biggest laugh making bathroom noises.

Normally Andrew would have appreciated their talents. Maybe even contributed. But at the moment, he was too busy trying to figure out what the heck the deal was with Eve. This whole night had been like a roller coaster. They'd had so much fun at the park. The car ride had been so easy. But the next thing he knew, she'd gotten mad at him for looking at her. Literally *looking* at her—the same way he had a gazillion times before. And then, just when they got past that and started having fun again, Holden showed up and ruined everything.

He'd *had* to grab her hand. Right? It was the only way he could think of to make Holden back off. Maybe it was a little weird. But it wasn't like he and Eve hadn't arm wrestled a thousand times. It really wasn't much different from that. Except he felt like it kind of was. Because she'd pulled away so fast and literally run out of the room. Andrew wondered if she would come back or if she was already halfway home. He felt sick to his stomach.

Everything was such a mess, and it felt to Andrew like whatever he did just made it worse. Like he was ruining the relationship that was most important to him, and he didn't know how to stop.

Ramirez called, "Exploding toilet," before making an elaborate series of noises that sounded pretty much exactly the way Andrew felt.

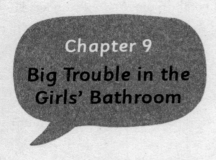

Chapter 9
Big Trouble in the Girls' Bathroom

The bathroom, Eve reflected, was the closest thing the muggle world had to a Room of Requirement. She had come there looking for a hiding spot. But she walked in on one girl weeping into a brown paper towel and another one cleaning post-cry mascara streaks off her face. Clearly the bathroom was already being used as a trauma recovery room. Their friends were there too, offering sympathy and advice—so it was also a counseling center.

Weeping Girl's friend shushed her like a baby, patting her back.

Eve went to one of the sinks and slowly, methodically began to wash her hands. It was the only way to hang out in here without going into a stall for way too long. There was no way Eve was doing *that*. Aside from the grossness factor of a school toilet, there was the public humiliation. If there was anything worse than someone suddenly announcing to the whole room that you were someone's *girlfriend*, it was a bunch of people thinking you were pooping.

She let the water run over her fingers.

"I can*not* believe he was flirting with his ex after he came here with *you*. Of *course* you're upset," Mascara Girl's friend said.

"Guys are the worst," Mascara Girl said to the mirror.

"So what are you going to do?" her friend asked.

"Like, seriously, ignore him for the rest of the dance." She jammed her blackened paper towel into the trash, pulled a tube of mascara from her mini backpack, and started applying a fresh coat.

She came equipped for this?! Eve was both impressed at the girl's Eagle Scout–level preparedness and concerned for the girl's emotional well-being. Who *plans* to cry at a school event?

Behind them, Weeping Girl blew her nose loudly and got a new paper towel.

The faucet timed out, and Eve pushed it down again.

"I've never seen anyone wash their hands that long," Mascara Girl commented, leaning over so her nose was inches from the mirror and brushing her lashes with the wand. Eve braced herself for a snide remark. But the girl said, "Avoiding someone?"

"Yeah," Eve admitted. When she said it out loud like that, it sounded so pathetic. She *hated* that she was hiding from Andrew. Who hides from their best friend?

"Well, hope it all works out!" The girl dropped her mascara into her purse, and she and her friend left the bathroom.

There was another deep sob from Weeping Girl, another *shhh* from her friend. Eve slowly pressed the pump on the pink soap. How had this situation gotten away from her? Andrew must have gotten the wrong impression . . . somehow. Eve shuddered. She knew exactly how he'd gotten that impression. She'd been blowing up his phone with kissy faces and heart eyes and ushy-gushy texts for two weeks. Every time her mom had a new idea about the Big Date, Eve would say, "I'll text Andrew!" It made her mom so happy to plan the outfits and the matching shoes and the golden hour photo shoot. But now Eve realized she had taken it too far. He thought she *liked him* liked him, and it was all her fault.

She had to tell him they were just friends. Right away. Before this got even weirder. She would go out there, find Andrew, and just tell him she was *not* his girlfriend.

Weeping Girl wailed, "What kind of person friendzones someone *at a dance*?!" For a panicked moment, Eve thought the girl was yelling at *her*. But the girl went on, "He could have texted me tomorrow or something. Like, just let me be happy for *one night*."

Okay, thought Eve, *new plan.* She would play along for tonight and text him in the morning.

She turned the water on again, watching each soap bubble as it slid away.

She definitely didn't want to hurt Andrew's feelings. She didn't want him crying in the bathroom or anything. Did guys even do that—cry in the bathroom? Anyway, the point was, she wasn't a monster. She would clear this up tomorrow.

Decision made, soap bubbles annihilated, and heart rate back to normal, Eve grabbed a paper towel. As Weeping Girl's sobs got calmer, the bathroom door opened, and Reese and Destiny stormed in.

"Oh my gosh, *that* guy!" Destiny said. She noticed Eve and said, "Hey!"

Reese's head tilted. "Yeah, but did you see Jamal looking at me?"

Eve's parents used to watch a ton of political dramas. So she recognized the look on Reese's face. It was the face that brilliant politicians made when some complicated thing played out just how they'd planned. So the bathroom was a war room now too.

Reese nodded to herself in the mirror. "He wants me back."

"Are you going to get back with him?" Destiny asked.

Reese shrugged. "Depends on how much he grovels, I guess. Like, I don't *need* him. But I still *like* him."

Destiny turned to Eve, concern in her eyes. "What are *you* doing in here? You okay?"

"Yeah," Eve said. "Just washing my hands."

"Good," Reese said, sounding relieved. "Because we'll all be gutted if Evedrew ever breaks up."

"Ever?" Eve parroted.

"Well—" Destiny pursed her lips. "I mean, live your life. But if *you* break up with *him*, we're gonna be like 'What the actual heck?' 'Cuz he's literally the cutest thing, and the way he looks at you—"

"*Seriously.* That *look.* I could die."

"Oh. Okay," Eve said, pulling open the door. "See you back out there."

They were just being funny, she told herself. Her friends wouldn't actually get mad at her over this. Besides, she wasn't technically breaking up with him since they were never really dating in the first place. She was simply clearing up a misunderstanding.

In the hall outside the bathroom, Nina had Brendan by the sleeve. Her voice was scathing. "—even come to this dance with me?! Did you seriously think I wanted to hang out with your friends all night?!"

Brendan matched her angry tone. "What's your problem with my friends?"

Eve rushed past, head down. She'd had all the drama she could take for one night. She briefly considered texting her mom that she wanted to leave early. But then she pictured the disappointment—no the *devastation*—on her mom's face if she thought the Big Date hadn't gone well. Her dad would probably say something about "not putting too much pressure on the kids," and the whole thing would blow up. Eve was *not* going to give her parents another reason to fight. She would shut this dance down if it killed her.

She just needed to find Andrew, eat some dang Takis, and play along. *It's fine,* thought Eve. *It's only one night.*

She scanned the gym and found Andrew. He had loosened his tie, rolled up his shirtsleeves, and messed up the tidy *swoop* of his dark hair. It should have made him look like a slob, but it did *not*. He looked breathtaking—like someone she'd be lucky to be seen with.

But he was still surrounded by his drumline crew. Her shoulders slumped. Now she understood why Nina was upset with Brendan. Eve hadn't realized that coming to the dance with Andrew meant she had to hang out with his friends, too. They were fine as far as a bunch of boys went, she guessed, but they weren't her friend group.

With a sigh of resignation, Eve dragged herself toward the guys.

Andrew greeted her with a "hey."

Then Jamal made a noise like gushing water, and Mateo laughed so hard that Eve thought he was going to fall onto the floor. Arav turned purple and had a coughing fit into his elbow. *It seriously wasn't that funny,* thought Eve.

From the corner of her eye, she saw Nina leaning against the wall with her arms crossed.

Pointedly turning her back on the noisemakers, Eve told Andrew, "Um, something happened and Nina kind of needs me. So. I'll see you later. Okay?"

Andrew mumbled something that Eve assumed meant yes, and she made her escape. She didn't go within ten feet of the boys again. She glued herself to Nina, Destiny, Reese, and Sofia—not acknowledging Andrew's frequent glances her way—until, one by one, people started trickling out. When she and Sofia were the only ones left, she started to get nervous. What would she do if they left her alone? Would she be forced to go back and hang out with the guys? Thankfully, her phone buzzed with a text from her mom.

Mom

I'm here!

64

After saying goodbye to Sofia, Eve collected Andrew with an arm wave and a "Mom's here." She didn't wait for him while he traded *see ya*s and *later, bruh*s with the other guys. Just kept walking. He caught up with her at the door, which she pushed through before he had a chance to open it for her.

"Eve?" Andrew asked.

Eve heard what he was really saying: *What's going on?* But since she couldn't friendzone him until tomorrow, she just smiled and opened the car door for him, bowing like a butler. He scratched his head, like he always did when he was uncomfortable or confused, but got into the car without asking any questions. Eve slid in next to him, making sure she had her whole skirt inside the car before closing the door.

"How was the dance?" Mom asked with a yawn.

Then Eve remembered what she was doing all this for. She threaded her hand around Andrew's arm and smiled hugely into the rearview mirror. "It was super fun! Right, Andrew?"

"Uhhh." Andrew shot her one more questioning look, and then said, "Yeah. It was great."

"Great!" Mom parroted.

"Great." Eve sighed, suddenly exhausted from playing so many parts. The girls, the guys, her mom, Andrew . . . All night she'd been twisting and turning to make sure they each saw only the version of her that they wanted to see.

She wished she could talk to her best friend about the whole mess. It would be such a relief to laugh about the whole boyfriend-girlfriend weirdness and be done with it. Eve released Andrew's arm and folded her hands in her lap.

A couple of minutes later, they were home. Andrew didn't try to open the door for her. He didn't ask any questions. He just said, "Thank you for driving us, Mrs. McNeil," mumbled, "See ya later" to Eve, and got out of the car. Eve watched him amble down the driveway, scrubbing at his hair.

Tomorrow. She'd tell him tomorrow.

Chapter 10
Partake of the Waffles of Wisdom

Andrew tapped paradiddles on the counter while he waited for his frozen waffles to pop out of the toaster. It was Thursday morning, and he was still trying to figure out what had happened at the dance on Saturday. After the Holden thing, Eve had spent the rest of the night hanging out with the other Cross Country girls. He thought maybe she was mad, and she definitely didn't seem like she wanted him to come over near her friends. But then she'd been all smiley and touchy-feely when they left. So maybe ditching a guy at a dance was just a normal thing for a girl to do?

He knew she wouldn't text him first thing the next day. She always went for a run on Sunday mornings. But he thought she'd text him *sometime* so they could get past the dance weirdness. When she didn't, he texted her. And she did text back. But her overexcited emojis had turned into one-word responses, which dwindled into fewer and fewer letters. **Idk . . . cu . . . k.**

At school she wouldn't even look at him. Talking was completely out of the question. So now they'd been officially dating for five days, and she was ignoring him harder than ever, if that was possible.

He hated this. He wanted his friend back. Just thinking about it made him want to cry.

Andrew almost jumped out of his skin when a cold, wet lump smacked him in the back of the neck. His hand went instinctively to the spot, making contact with a milk-soaked shredded wheat, as he whirled around to see his brother with his spoon in catapult mode.

"The heck?!" Andrew snarled, throwing the blob into the sink so hard, it splattered.

Tom grinned. "I said your name, like, five times."

"What do you want?" The waffles popped up, and Andrew juggled them onto his plate, only burning his fingers a little.

"Dude, why you being such a grouch?"

Andrew clattered his plate onto the table and threw himself into a chair. "Aside from the fact that I'm probably going to smell like sour milk all day—"

"Come on, that was an amazing shot. Just admit you're impressed."

"—I can't figure out this thing with Eve." Andrew shoved half a waffle into his mouth.

"The dating thing? What's to figure out?"

Andrew made an "I don't know" sound with his mouth full, swallowed, and said, "Maybe why it sucks."

Tom laughed. "Seriously?"

"*Seriously*. Should I text her that I just want to be friends again?"

"Only if you *never* want to be friends again."

"*WHAT?!*"

Tom made a face like he couldn't believe how naïve Andrew was. "Girls love to friendzone people. It's like a hobby. But Kenna went full honey badger when I friendzoned her. She—"

"You friendzoned Kenna?"

"Bruh, focus." Tom grimaced. "I'm telling you, if you friendzone Eve, she will hate you forever."

"Then what am I supposed to do?" Andrew demanded.

Tom shrugged. "I promise you, if you want any hope of being friends again, you've got to wait for *her* to break up with *you*."

Andrew felt like someone was crashing cymbals inside his head. "What if she doesn't, though?"

"Try being super annoying. That should be easy for you." Tom scooped a huge bite of cereal into his mouth and grinned. Andrew scowled. With his mouth still full, Tom added, "Wha? You were besties, right? Don't you know all her pet peeves?"

Andrew would never admit it out loud under any kind of torture tactic, but his big brother was right. He knew *exactly* how to annoy Eve. Maybe he really could fix this whole situation by getting Eve to dump him. In a few days, everything could go back to normal. He polished off his second waffle feeling better than he had in days.

"Binary stars orbit each other like this," Ms. Medgar explained, using her coffee cup and a donut hole to demonstrate. "But sometimes they get *too* close. Remember, these two stars were born in the same nebula. They're basically brother and sister. But as they circle each other, the smaller, denser star begins to steal energy from the other star. Like a greedy, hungry baby, it gobbles up more and more of the big star."

Eve watched in horrified fascination as the donut hole circled closer and closer to the cup. She was supposed to be taking notes, but her pencil dangled limply from her fingers.

"Spoiler alert—there's going to be a supernova." Ms. Medgar paused. "Can anyone guess why?"

Hands shot up around the room.

"Kyle?"

"I'm guessing the smaller star eventually eats so much it explodes?"

"Mmmm, good guess. But it's even *weirder*." Ms. Medgar's voice hushed, like she was telling them a secret. "Eventually, the smaller star steals so much energy that what used to be the bigger star becomes a white dwarf." She swapped out her coffee mug for a Tic Tac. "And collapses in on itself! *BOOM!*"

The end-of-the-day bell rang in perfect timing with the supernova, making Eve jump. Notebooks slammed shut and conversations broke out all around her.

Ms. Medgar called over the cacophony, "Expect a quiz tomorrow!" She popped the Tic Tac into her mouth.

Eve slowly closed her notebook and tucked her pencil back into the NASA pencil pouch Andrew had given her for her twelfth birthday.

"You okay, Eve?"

She looked up and realized she was the last one in the room. Ms. Medgar was looking at her with one eyebrow up, crunching pensively on her Tic Tac. If Eve didn't hurry, she'd be late for Cross Country, and Coach Watkins would make her do push-ups. She hated push-ups.

Eve stood but didn't leave. "Um, Ms. Medgar?"

"Yeah?"

"Isn't there any way for the two stars *not* to destroy each other?"

The teacher's head quirked to the side. Her lips tipped up. "Sure. If they're just a little farther apart, the system stays stable. But gravity is always pulling them toward each other. It's a cosmic dance."

Eve's calves itched. *Poor stars,* she thought. *Destined to suck the life out of each other because of stupid gravity that's totally outside of their control.* Aloud she said, "Well, I've gotta go to practice. See you tomorrow." She tucked her notebook under her arm and ran.

Coach Watkins made her do fifteen push-ups. Then the whole team set out on a three-mile neighborhood run. As soon as they were out of Coach's sight, the pack's pace slowed to an easy jog.

"I hate boys," Nina announced.

"Like, all boys? Or just Brendan?" Destiny asked.

"Mostly Brendan. But also all boys." She cut her gaze to Eve. "No offense."

"None taken," Eve muttered, too caught up in her own thoughts to know why she should be offended. She could still picture the doomed stars orbiting each other as her brain circled the same problem she'd been stuck on for five days. She just had to figure out how to untangle herself from Andrew before this whole thing went supernova.

Every day since the dance, she'd planned on breaking things off. And every day she couldn't do it. The biggest problem was her mom. The morning after the dance, when she got back from her run, Eve had been composing her friendzone text to Andrew when her mom had walked in and said, "Who're you texting?"

"Andrew," Eve had said, not even looking up. She had erased and restarted the text so many times, trying to come up with the nicest way to do it. Version 3.2b was: **Sorry if that was weird last night. You were just joking about the girlfriend thing, right?** She reread it and then decided to add: **I'm so glad we're just friends**. She chewed her lip and changed "so" to "really."

And then her mom had sighed, "*You two.* You remind me what it's like when things are new and fresh." Eve thought she heard her mom's voice catch, and she looked up. Mom sniffed. "I miss that feeling."

Eve erased the text.

The next night at dinner, her mom had asked how Andrew was. When Eve blushed and stammered because she hadn't talked to him at all since the hand-holding disaster, her dad had said accusingly, "You're embarrassing her, Jo."

"I just asked a question," Mom shot back.

"You're putting too much pressure on the kids," Dad insisted.

Mom's lips pressed together, and her eyes flared.

Eve blurted, "Andrew's great! *We're* great! Everything's great."

Mom's face had relaxed, and she said, "You know, you can invite him over for dinner anytime."

Dad hadn't said anything else.

Eve shook her head at the memory. If she told the truth about not wanting to date Andrew, she might as well file her parents' divorce papers herself. And then there was the Eve-drew fan club—Destiny and Reese had basically said they'd hate her if she broke up with Andrew. So Eve was trapped. She couldn't stop being Andrew's girlfriend even though it was sucking the life out of her.

If dating were fun—just like being friends but more official—she might feel differently. But it wasn't. It was *way worse* than anything she could have imagined. Mostly they just avoided each other at school and sporadically texted like strangers.

At least there hadn't been any more long looks or hand-holding attempts. Andrew didn't seem any more excited about this boyfriend-girlfriend thing than she felt. *Maybe he'll break up with me,* Eve thought with a glimmer of hope. That would solve *everything*. No one would blame her if she was the one who got dumped. Her mom and dad would feel so bad for her that they wouldn't want to make it worse by fighting. Eve might be able to play the "I can't take any more heartbreak" card and convince her parents to play nice for weeks . . . months maybe.

The more Eve thought about Andrew dumping her, the more excited she got. She wouldn't have to hurt his feelings, and they could go back to being best friends! It was really the perfect solution. The only problem was, he was a super chill guy. Outside of drumline—and that hand grab at the dance—he mostly just let life happen. If she left it up to him, Andrew might drag this out until they were middle-aged. She had a feeling it would take more than minor ghosting to get him to make a move.

As they came up to a crosswalk, Eve realized she had outpaced the pack of girls. Only Nina jogged in place next to her, waiting for the light to change. Nina, who, at the moment, mostly hated all boys. Nina, who was a take-charge kind of girl.

"Hey, Nina," Eve ventured.

"Yeah?"

"If I ask you something, will you promise not to tell anyone?"

"Okay?"

"Seriously, not Destiny or Reese or *anyone*."

"What's up?"

The WALK sign lit, and both girls started across the street. As they ran, Eve said, "Theoretically, if someone *wanted* a guy to break up with them, what do you think she should do?"

Nina scoffed. "*Theoretically* tell the guy where he can stick his immature friends and his cheap body spray on his way out the door."

"But what if, because of reasons, she *can't* tell him off? He just has to break up with her and not the other way around?" Eve pressed.

"Hmmm." Nina considered it, eyes on the horizon as she ran. "It depends. How far is this theoretical girl willing to go to get herself dumped?"

Eve kept pace with her teammate, eyes on the road. There was no point in pretending they both didn't know who they were talking about. She said, "I don't want to do anything that will get me suspended or anything. And I don't want to hurt Andrew's feelings—just make him see that us dating is a terrible, horrible, awful idea."

Nina laughed. "Oh, girl. This is going to be *fun*."

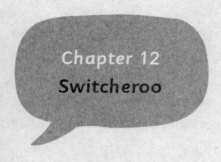

Chapter 12
Switcheroo

Andrew was keyed up Friday morning. He drummed on his legs the whole way to school. He'd spent all of yesterday making a mental list of Eve's pet peeves and working himself up to actually doing them. The thing was, he had never made Eve mad on purpose before. On accident, sure. But he'd hated it every time—hated when her smile disappeared, hated how she wouldn't quite look at him and the way her voice got tight.

This getting-Eve-to-dump-him plan had seemed like such a good idea when Tom came up with it. But the prospect of facing a whole day of Eve's anger (it couldn't take more than a day, could it?) made Andrew a little queasy.

The first problem was that he and Eve hardly had any

classes together. In order to annoy her, he had to *find* her. He'd gotten here early so he could look for her before his first-hour science class. His plan was to check the cafeteria. They sold bagels and fruit juice and stuff before school, and a lot of the sportsy kids hung out in there. Andrew figured it was because they were constantly carb-loading.

When he got to the cafeteria, he skirted the edges, feeling awkward. Andrew didn't hang out with any of these kids, and he felt like he didn't belong here. He had the gut feeling that if he could find Eve, everything would be okay. His brain knew that wasn't true anymore, but a few weeks of weirdness couldn't override instincts built from a lifetime of Eve being his safe person. *I didn't lose her,* Andrew told himself. *We'll be friends again by tomorrow.*

He didn't see Eve, but he did spot Destiny and Reese with some of the other Cross Country girls. With the same feeling he'd had the first time he'd forced himself to jump off the high dive at the public pool, Andrew pushed away from the wall and headed toward them. *This is it,* he thought. *Operation Eve's Pet Peeves is a go.*

"HEY," he said over the din to get their attention.

"ANDREW!" Destiny greeted him with way more enthusiasm than he deserved.

"Hi, Destiny," he said, "Have you seen Eve?"

There was a chorus of "Aaaaaaaw" from a couple of the

other girls, like him looking for Eve had the same cuteness factor as a litter of puppies. But Destiny said, "She and Nina went looking for *you*."

"Really?!" Andrew was floored. Eve *never* looked for him at school. Maybe she was already breaking up with him!

"Yeah," Destiny confirmed. "I think they were heading toward the band room."

Andrew said thanks before ambling out of the room. As soon as the cafeteria doors closed behind him, he took off running toward the band room. There were only a few minutes left before the first bell.

He came up behind Nina and Eve in the fine arts hall, and realized he *needed* to intercept them before they got to the band room. Otherwise, he'd have to get Eve to dump him with all his friends watching. The thought made him feel hot all over and slightly nauseous. He'd been so focused on how good it would feel to get out of this dating thing that he hadn't thought about the humiliation of getting publicly dumped. He really hoped the guys wouldn't make a big deal about it. *But even if they do,* he assured himself, *it will still be worth it to get Eve's friendship back.*

He forced himself to walk forward, clearing his throat to get the girls' attention. Nina glanced back and jostled Eve. They both turned to face him. Suddenly he was up on that high-dive platform again. *Don't look. Just jump.*

"Hi, Eve!" He tried to sound excited, but his voice cracked, which made him sound nervous or possibly just weird.

"Oh, *hiiiiii*, Aaaaandrew," Eve said.

What the what?! Ever since the start of eighth grade, Eve's number one unspoken rule had been: *There is no "us" at school.* No talking, no waving, no eye contact. He'd only come looking for her because he knew it would make her furious. Her completely wrong reaction threw him off—he had no idea what to do next. He should stick to the plan, right?

Right.

If he upped the tempo, she was sure to crack.

Andrew gritted his teeth and looked at Eve—right at her, long and hard. He hoped it was a gaze and not a glare. He had no idea what his face was doing at this point.

Whatever it was, it worked. Eve looked mortified. Her feet twitched on the linoleum. He already had a plan for this—if she ran, he would follow her, calling her name. She would probably dump him on the spot. He smiled a little at the thought. This was almost too easy.

But she didn't run. Instead, when Nina jabbed her in the ribs, she took a step toward him, arranged her face into an unnatural smile, and fluttered her eyelashes.

Andrew felt his eyes go wide. Who was this person, and what had she done to his friend?

Eve said in a too-high voice, "I was just looking for you to see if you want to sit together at lunch today."

Should he say yes? On one hand, more time together meant more chances to be annoying. But if she *wanted* to sit with him, then what was the point? Plus he always sat with the drumline guys. He didn't want to abandon his friends. He said, "Uh."

Eve's eyelashes fluttered even harder. It looked so silly that, under any other circumstances, Andrew would have laughed out loud. But it also made him realize he needed more time to think through his plan. The rules had obviously changed when he wasn't looking. He cleared his throat and willed his voice not to crack again. "I'm, uh, sitting with the guys."

Eve looked relieved.

"Oh, that's okay," Nina chimed in, pushing Eve closer to him. "She'd love to sit with all the guys! *Right*, Eve?"

"Right?" Eve mumbled.

"Right!" Nina cheered.

"Riiiight." Andrew blew out a defeated breath. Round one—Eve. "So I guess I'll . . . see you at lunch."

"'Kay," Eve agreed.

Nina cleared her throat loudly.

"Give me your hoodie!" Eve practically shouted, the way people in movies shout *Put your hands up!*

Andrew froze. "Huh?"

Nina chimed in again, "She means that she wants to wear your hoodie so she can think about you every minute between now and then."

"Oh." Andrew suddenly felt itchy all over. He scratched his arm and then his ribs and then his hair. He was wearing his brand-new LJHS Marching Band hoodie, and he couldn't even remember what T-shirt he had put on under it. What if it had pit stains and ketchup on it? Besides, it felt kind of weird to take some of his clothes off in the hallway.

Eve held out a hand expectantly, and Andrew didn't know how to refuse without making this whole situation more awkward than it already was. Feeling like he was moving through water, he set down his backpack, took hold of the hem of his hoodie, and lifted it. He glanced down and was relieved to see his Sour Patch Kids T-shirt. That one wasn't too bad. He pulled his hoodie the rest of the way over his head. But then he hesitated. What if Eve lost it or got something on it? What if she didn't give it back after they broke up? What if he was cold?

Eve clutched the wadded fabric and pulled. For a second or two he resisted, and they were locked in a tug-of-war. But then he was afraid it would rip, so he let go. And just like that, the hoodie was hers. The whole thing felt like how he imagined being mugged would feel.

Eve looked down at the sweatshirt and then back up. Her foot tapped. Then she threw herself at him and hugged him, still clutching the hoodie in one hand. She put both arms around him and laid her cheek on his shoulder. He almost hugged her back—mostly from muscle memory and only a tiny bit because hugging Eve just felt *right*. But this situation was way too bizarro to do anything but stand with his arms pinned to his sides. "I'll *miss* you," she said in that weirdly high voice that made him sure she didn't mean it.

I've been *missing you,* came the whisper from Andrew's subconscious, and his heart squeezed in affirmation. He reminded himself that the only way to get their friendship back was to obliterate this dating thing. Whatever was going on with Eve today, he'd regroup and find a way to make her dump him.

The five-minute bell rang, and people started trickling out of the band room.

Andrew stepped out of the hug and swung his backpack onto his shoulder. "I'd better get to science." He whirled around and started walking before Eve could ambush him with any more mushy looks or demands for clothing.

"Andrew!" she called after him.

Reluctantly, he turned.

"Don't forget there's a quiz in science. So just, um, make sure to look over your notes." She stood there holding his hoodie and scrunching her nose like she always did when she was thinking. His heart squeezed again, maybe because this felt like the first honest moment between them since the dance. Maybe because she was looking out for him—like friends do.

"Okay, thanks," he mumbled before escaping around the corner.

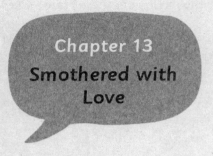

Chapter 13
Smothered with Love

As soon as Andrew was out of sight, Eve collapsed against the wall, still clutching his hoodie. "That was the worst," she said.

"Nuh-uh," Nina countered. "Being stuck at a dance for four hours with Brendan the human fart machine is the worst. You and Andrew are only, like, a grande hot mess with a double shot of awkward."

"Thanks?"

Nina held out her hand and wiggled her fingers. "Put on the hoodie and give me your phone."

Eve obeyed. Feeling like she knew where this was going, she said from inside the cozy fabric, "Can't post a pic, though. Neither one of us is allowed to have social media." She got the too-big hoodie over her head and pushed the sleeves up to free her hands. It smelled like Andrew, and it was still warm from his body heat. It really was like wearing a hug. Eve had been very against the "take his hoodie" part of the plan, because she'd always thought girls were just being silly about wearing their boyfriends' clothes. But now she understood why this was a thing.

Nina thought for a second. "Okay," she admitted, "that's a setback, but we can still work with it." She snapped a picture of Eve. "We'll send it to the group chat."

"What group chat?" Eve asked.

"The one from his nightmares. The one I'm about to make with all the girls and his homies."

Eve shook her head. "I don't have any of their numbers."

"We'll get them." Nina handed back the phone and motioned for them to start walking. "Look, this is important. If you're going to smother him, you have to commit."

The thing is, Eve *didn't* want to smother him. She hated torturing Andrew. Eve grabbed her backpack off the floor and jogged to catch up next to Nina. "Nina, what if . . ." She mentally searched for a way out and came up with, "What if I just talk to Andrew and, you know, explain that I didn't mean to give him the wrong idea before, and I don't want to be his girlfriend?"

"Yeah!" Nina cheered and pumped her fist. "But can I just be there when you do it? I love to watch boys cry!"

"What?!"

Nina gave her a *duh* look. "Well, that's pretty much the cruelest thing you could do. Especially because he obviously has it *bad* for you. But, I mean, I'm into it."

"No, that's not—I don't want to hurt his feelings, remember?"

"Then definitely don't try to *talk* to him. Boys can't handle that. At all. *Trust me.*"

"Okay," Eve sighed, defeated. "You're right. I'll smother him." *It's the kindest thing you can do,* she told herself. Just like she and Nina had already decided—he would get to think she liked him *too* much, and he would be the one to end it. His fragile boy ego would stay completely intact. He'd be over this weird crush or whatever it was, and they could get back to laughing and having fun like normal people.

Eve jogged to keep up with Nina. "But how much longer do you think . . . until he dumps me?"

"Smothering takes a while. Probably at least a week. Boys are pretty clueless. You gotta play the long game." Nina assured her, "It'll work. You know what you need to do at lunch, right?"

"Yeah," Eve said. She wished Nina had the same lunch as her and Andrew, because she really did want backup. Knowing what she needed to do was one thing, but actually doing it was way harder than she'd thought it would be. Flirting and fawning and acting all giggly and swoony . . . it just wasn't the real her. She was certain Andrew—who knew her better than anyone else on the planet—could see right through her act. But she and Nina had a plan for that, too. If he called her on it, she'd burst out crying and accuse him of hating her. If he didn't call her on it, she would just keep smothering him until he couldn't take it anymore.

Nina had assured her that "smothering" was the number one cause for boys dumping people. So she was going to full-on suffocate Andrew.

Thankfully, Eve was pretty good at compartmentalizing. For the first three hours of the day, she focused in class, took good notes, and finished her math work early. It was true that every couple of minutes she got a whiff of Andrew's sweatshirt or noticed the soft brush of the hoodie against her neck, but that wasn't because she *liked* him. She didn't have chills or anything. If anything, she had a warm fuzzy feeling. Until she remembered the messed-up situation they were in and that the only way out of it was to make him hate her.

Temporarily.

Later, he would thank her, and they'd laugh about this.

But what if he didn't?

That one anxious thought was what made her feel so queasy as she weaved through the cafeteria with her insulated lunch bag. Before making her way to Andrew's table, she stopped to say hi to Sofia, Destiny, and Reese.

"Hey, girl!" they all sang in unison.

Sofia said, "Oh my gosh, is that Andrew's hoodie?! It's so, so, so sweet that he gave it to you!"

"Yeah," Eve said noncommittally, remembering the look on his face when she'd demanded it. It was one part *heck no* and one part *who are you?* But he'd given it to her anyway, because he was sweet like that. Yeah, she'd basically torn it out of his hand. But she knew he had let her win.

Eve realized she was scrunching her nose and forced her face back to neutral, saying, "So anyway, I'm going to sit with Andrew today. Sorry to abandon you guys."

The girls gave her a chorus of "It's okay" and "No worries." And then it was time for Eve to go to the place and do the thing.

She tried to make her trudge look like a hip-swaying catwalk, like Nina had shown her. She had no idea if she was pulling it off, but about halfway there the boys started noticing her approach. They turned to watch her, and she heard Mateo Ramirez say, "Bruh, your girlfriend's incoming."

"Yeah." Andrew shrugged. "She's sitting with us, I guess. It's no big deal."

Andrew's obvious discomfort with her joining his friend group sparked new hope and determination in Eve. Nina was right! This was working!

For the first time since sixth grade—when it had become basically illegal to sit mixed-gender in the lunchroom—she put her lunch bag down next to Andrew's. She offered a smile to the whole table as she wedged herself into the tiny space next to him, forcing Arav Kumari to scoot over to make room. "Hi, guys!" she said brightly.

There was a round of heys before they went back to stuffing their faces. Eve got out an apple and a deli wrap, purposely leaning into Andrew so that it was impossible for him to use his right arm without jostling her. Every time he lifted his hand to his mouth, he shot her a look that was part *sorry* and part *personal space please*.

She counted to fifteen in her head and then said, "Oops, Andy Wandy. You have something"—she pointed to the corner of her mouth—"just right there."

Andrew cringed at the hated nickname.

Jamal scoffed. "Andy Wandy?" he said under his breath. Perfect.

Andrew swiped a hand across his mouth, looking like he wanted to crawl under the table.

"Almost. Nope, it's still there. Let me." Eve took her napkin and dabbed at the nonexistent food on Andrew's face. He leaned away and turned his head, but she just leaned with him, relentless. The other guys couldn't contain their sniggers, which made a nervous laugh bubble up in Eve, too. She pressed her lips together to hold it in, trying to make it look pouty. One more dab, and then she said, "All better now, sweetums."

Arav choked on his sports drink. Jamal snorted.

Eve turned on them, doing her best to look indignant. "You guys, don't laugh at my Andy! He's sensitive. You'll hurt his feelings!"

"It's fine," Andrew growled, glaring at his sandwich.

"No it's not!" Eve insisted loudly. "If these guys are mean to you, I don't think it's healthy for you to hang out with them."

"What?!" Andrew coughed.

"Girl, chill," Jamal said.

Eve slapped her hand against her chest. "Andy! Are you going to let him talk to me like that?"

"Uh." Andrew visibly struggled to find words. "It's fine. You're just being . . ." He trailed off.

"WHAT, *Andy*?! What am I being?" Eve screeched.

She was giddy. This was going perfectly—and way faster than Nina had predicted. Andrew narrowed his eyes in rage, and she was sure he was going to break up with her here and now.

He said, "You probably just have low blood sugar. Here." He shoved a spoonful of chocolate pudding into her mouth, smiling maliciously. "How's that, *sweetums*?"

Eve was stunned for a second. Other people putting food into her mouth was pretty much the thing Eve hated most in the world. Andrew knew that. She had obviously pushed him too far. But why not just *break up* with her, then?

She managed not to spit the pudding out—just barely. With great effort, she swallowed and growled, "Thanks."

Everyone at the table looked like they wanted to be anywhere else but here. No one made eye contact. Everyone fidgeted.

Finally Mateo blurted, "What's everybody going as for Halloween?"

Eve couldn't help but appreciate him for the subject change. Maybe boys weren't as clueless as Nina said.

Arav jumped in with visible relief. "I'm getting a fuzzy dinosaur costume."

"Classic," Jamal said. "I'm going as a frat boy. I'm just gonna hold a red cup."

Mateo burst out laughing. "That's hilarious."

"What's yours?" Jamal asked.

Mateo said, "Ima be a plague doctor."

"What about you, Andrew?" Arav asked.

Eve saw an opportunity to level up her smothering exponentially. *He'll thank me later,* she reminded herself, jumping in before Andrew had a chance to answer. "We're going to do a couples costume!"

If she had smacked him in the face with her deli wrap, Andrew could not have looked more surprised and disgusted. She took his arm with both hands, swallowing her own embarrassment. "Right, Andy Wandy? How about Tarzan and Jane?"

He shook his head, clearly too horrified for words.

"Belle and Beast?" She almost gagged on the words. It was so ridiculous.

He gave her a visual *Kill me now.*

"Okay, whatever," Jamal said. "Anyway, my mom said she'd drive us to the neighborhood with the good candy."

"Oh yeah! Charles Street—" Arav exclaimed.

"Full-sized Snickers last year!" Mateo slapped his hand on the table.

Eve could hear Nina's voice in her head insisting, *Smother him, girl. No mercy.* Ignoring her own conscience, she pasted on a not-sorry smile and said in a syrupy sweet tone, "Oh, Andy can't go with you guys, sorry. We're doing our own thing on Halloween."

"Really, *Andy Wandy*?!" Jamal was clearly losing his temper. "You're ditching us for a girl?"

Andrew looked from Jamal to Eve a few times. His mouth opened and closed. *Say it,* Eve thought at him. *Say you want to break up.*

Without a word, Andrew scooped up what was left of his lunch, pushed himself off the bench and away from the table, and stomped out of the lunchroom. Eve was left to look awkwardly around at the rest of the guys, knowing she'd won a battle but feeling like she'd lost something much more precious.

Chapter 14
Smells Like Revenge

Andrew spent the rest of the day replaying the lunch disaster in his head. It was so confusing. First Eve asked him out, then she started going hot and cold, and now she seemed to be purposely embarrassing him in front of his friends. Was she just joking, and he was taking things too seriously?

He could think of plenty of times when she'd called him Andy or Drew or even Andrea when she was trash-talking—like in Nerf wars, pillow fights, and playground races. But she always had his back when it counted. Like in fifth grade when Mr. Gutierrez—who was, like, seven feet tall and super strict—kept calling him Andy. Andrew wasn't about to correct him. So Eve had gone up to him on the fifth day of school and said, "Mr. Gutierrez, his name is Andrew. That's what he goes by."

Maybe today she had been nervous about trying to fit in with the drumline guys. Maybe she was just trying too hard.

She *must* have been joking about the Halloween thing. Right? But what if she wasn't? There was no way he was going to wear a weird couples costume and miss out on trick-or-treating with his crew. He seriously *had* to get her to break up with him before Halloween.

But *how*? Obviously being mushy wasn't working. It had just made her even more mushy. She'd out-mushied him. Twice. She'd definitely won round two at lunch today. He had to think of something else.

Instead of taking notes in any of his afternoon classes, Andrew added to his list of Eve's pet peeves.

- moles with hairs growing out of them
- gross noises
- Adam and Eve jokes
- close talkers

The moment he turned his phone on after the final bell, Andrew saw he had a text from Eve. It was a photo of her wearing his hoodie. Her hair was messed up and her cheeks were flushed. Something about the picture reminded him of

one day last fall when they had spent a whole Saturday rak-
ing piles of leaves and jumping into them. At sunset they had
lain side by side in the leaves and waited for the fireflies to
come out. That was a good day.

"What are you smiling at?" Arav asked, jostling his
shoulder.

"Uh—"

Before Andrew could answer, his phone blew up.

555-0127

> OMG Andrew gave you his
> hoodie??????????

555-0192

> you guys are sooooooo cute.

Jamal

> How did you get this number?

Holden

> gurl looks 🔥

555-0186

> Evedrew 4EVAH 💜💜💜

Ramirez

🫤

555-0186

Nobody asked you mateo 😟 💀

"Wow," Arav said, holding up his own phone with the same messages. "Are you gonna respond?"

Andrew scratched his ear. "I don't know what to say. This is weird."

"Yeah," Arav agreed. "Want to go to band?"

Andrew put his phone in his pocket and fell into step beside Arav, grateful for his friend's practical approach to life. He never seemed to feel flustered like Andrew did most of the time.

Band practice was outside. The afternoon was chilly, and Andrew really wished he had his hoodie. The one Eve *stole*. He also wished the guys would stop calling him Andy in high, whiny voices. Even Madison at one point said, "Hey *Andy*, you're rushing the sweeps!"

If one more person called him Andy, he might break a mallet over their head.

After practice, as they put their kits away, Andrew checked his phone. Seventeen more ushy-gushy messages. The last few made him extra uncomfortable.

McNugget

> Andy, I miss you every second!!! 😍 What are you doing right now????

> HELLO???!!!

> Why aren't you texting me back??

> 👻 ??? 😵 😣 💔

> I'm not mad, okay??? Let's walk home together 🥺 😵

Up until this year, he and Eve had always walked home together. And up until about four hours ago, all he really wanted was to hang out with Eve again. Now the thought of walking home with her made his armpits start sweating.

Maybe he could rub armpit sweat on her.

Ramirez looked at his phone and made a barfing noise. Andrew didn't blame him.

"AAAAAAAAAAAAAAAANNN-DEEEEEEEEEE,"

Eve beckoned him from the band room door in the loudest, most babyish voice he'd ever heard.

"Aaaaaaaannn-deeeeeee," Jamal and Ramirez mimicked, rolling their eyes and jabbing each other with drumsticks. Madison mimed sticking her finger down her throat.

Andrew had to remind himself again why he couldn't just break up with Eve. Telling her he wanted to be friends wouldn't work. He had to show her that she shouldn't have a crush on him, in order to salvage their friendship. Plus there was Holden. Seriously, what was with the *gurl looks "fire"* text? Eve could legally change his name to Andy, and he still wouldn't leave her to deal with Holden on her own.

He stashed his mallets, shouldered his backpack, and joined Eve at the door. She took his arm with a big, unnatural smile. Andrew felt like he was under arrest or something. He half expected her to say, "You have the right to remain silent . . ."

As they approached the vending machines in the front lobby, he got an idea. More than an idea—a plan. Tom had told him *exactly* what girls hate. So he would do it all.

"Hold on. I need snacks," Andrew said, digging into his backpack for money. When he found some, he fed it to the machines and got a bag of Takis and a Sprite. He didn't offer Eve any, but she didn't seem to care. That was fine with Andrew. She'd care about the next part.

"So I had some more ideas for Halloween," Eve chattered as they left the building.

Andrew opened the Takis and crammed a handful in his mouth, making sure to chew as loudly as possible with his mouth open.

Eve acted like she didn't notice. But her eye twitched. Her voice was determinedly cheerful. "We could be the dogs from *Lady and the Tramp*. And I could draw a widdle bwack nose on you." She punctuated her baby talk by poking him in the nose. Andrew resisted the urge to swat her hand away. Eve kept pushing. "Or how about Peter Pan and Wendy? You'd look so cute in green tights!"

Andrew ignored her and noisily gulped half the Sprite.

Eve was clearly frustrated at his non-reaction. Her voice pitched higher and louder. "Oh, I know! You could be a baby, and I could be a rattle! You'd wear a diaper for me, right, snookums?"

Andrew knew this was his moment. He slung his arm around her, making sure her shoulder was pressed right into the sweatiest part of his armpit. He clamped his hand on her other arm so she couldn't get away from him. Then he turned his face to her and let loose the loudest, longest, stinkiest burp of his life.

"GROSS!" She threw herself out of his grip so hard that she smacked into a tree. She rubbed her elbow and glared at him. "NASTY!"

Andrew sucked the Taki dust off his fingers, smacking his lips. "This is just how guys are, *snookums*. Since we're dating now, you might as well get used to it."

Eve made a noise of supreme disgust, threw up her hands, and stomped away.

Andrew raised his Sprite to her retreating form before taking a celebratory swig. Round three—Andrew.

Chapter 15
The Universe Takes Sides

The stench of Andrew's burp clung to Eve like a living thing. And the shoulder of her hoodie (well, Andrew's hoodie)—it was literally damp with his hairy armpit sweat. Boy stink was worse than her post-run BO. So. Much. Worse.

She peeled the hoodie off, trying not to breathe or let it touch her skin.

Her so-called best friend was officially the most disgusting person in the universe. She could barely concentrate on putting her mental armor on and prepping to cross her parents' battlefield as she went into the house. Surprisingly, there was no sound of her parents fighting. It was eerily quiet.

"Hello?" she called.

"In here," came her dad's voice from the kitchen. Eve

went as far as the kitchen door and found him chopping vegetables. There was a half-empty bottle of beer on the counter. Dread swept over her.

Rockets have a maximum payload—the amount they can carry and still make it out of the atmosphere. The weight of Eve's constant anxiety about her parents felt like that max payload. Adding even the smallest thing—like a sudden disappearance or a beer before dinner—could make her entire life crash and burn.

"Where's Mom?" Eve asked, her voice sounding small and thin in her own ears.

"She and Babs—I mean Mrs. Ozdemir—decided to have a girls' night. It's just us for dinner." He sounded tired. Exhausted.

"Oh. Okay."

As she headed upstairs, Eve told herself to calm down. There was no emergency. Dad was just tired. Mom was just out with a friend . . . on a random school night.

When her phone chirped, she dug it out eagerly, happy for something to interrupt her thought spiral.

Nina Torpedo

> How did it go after school? Are you single yet??

It was exactly what she needed. Focusing on her disgust at Andrew was way better than fixating on her parents' issues. She dropped her backpack and immediately texted Nina the story of Andrew's bad behavior. Nina's response came in seconds.

Nina Torpedo

> OMG boys are so gross!! 😫

Eve

> I know 😵 ALSO I told all the guys that we had a THING for Halloween!! 😫 😱 WHAT DO I DO????

Nina Torpedo

> that's in like three weeks 🙃 hopefully you guys will break up before then

Eve

> Yeah but what if we don't??

Nina Torpedo

> We could do a haunted house, maybe.

Or maybe Destiny would do a bonfire.
They have a huge backyard!

Eve

Those would be so cool!

btw I said we're doing a couples costume 😳 😬 I told Andrew he should wear a diaper 🫨

Nina Torpedo

😂 😂 😂

u r awesome

Eve

What am I going to do?????????

I have to call it off.

Nina Torpedo

So keep dating him? Or break up with him?

NEITHER. Can I just crawl in a hole??

Nina Torpedo

ummmmm . . . no hole option. Just:

keep dating

dump him

make him wear a diaper

Eve buried her face in her pillow and groaned. What had she gotten herself into?

The next day was Saturday. It was Eve's least favorite day of the week because she was stuck at home with both her parents all day. There was no fighting today, for the first time Eve could remember. But it wasn't peace. It was the start of the cold war.

While she was eating toast with her dad, her mom came into the kitchen and headed straight for the coffeepot without

107

so much as saying good morning. Her dad immediately got up and left the room.

Her mom poured herself coffee as if Dad didn't even exist. Like she didn't notice he was ever there, let alone that he had left like he couldn't stand to be in the same room with her. Eve stared at her half-eaten toast, suddenly not hungry at all. Mom took her coffee back to her bedroom and slammed the door behind her.

It was *so much worse* than yelling.

Last year, she would have retreated to Andrew's house. They could have eaten his mom's amazing brownies and laughed about any random thing to take her mind off her problems.

Maybe she could still do it. Andrew wouldn't be gross on purpose if he knew she was dealing with all this. He would forgive her for being a jerk at lunch, and they could just go back to how it used to be, at least for this one day.

The chance for that was too good to pass up. She went to her room to get her phone so she could text him to ask if he was up yet. But she had a message from Nina:

Nina Torpedo

I HAVE LITERALLY THE BEST IDEA!!! MEET ME AT THE LIBRARY!

Eve texted back some question marks. Nina immediately responded.

Nina Torpedo

u r going to love me 4ever 😇

hurry up i'm already here

Twenty minutes later, Eve locked her bike to the bike rack at the library and went in search of Nina. She found her in the Teen Reading Room—a converted meeting room strewn with beanbag chairs and papered with quotes someone thought sounded relevant to teenagers. Even though the room was obviously trying too hard, Eve appreciated it if only for its TEENS ONLY sign on the door. There weren't that many places where people with no car and no house of their own could get away from constant adult prying.

Nina was sitting cross-legged on a beanbag against the far wall. When Eve walked in, she looked up from her book, grinned maniacally, and said, "Look at this."

She held up the book she had been reading. The cover said, *All the Tea: Talking, Dating, and True Love.* She crowed, "It's a dating advice book!"

Eve was a little confused about why this would make her love Nina forever. The last thing she really wanted was dating advice. She wanted to be *not* dating. Was there a book about that?

Nina held out the book. "Check out chapter three."

Eve plopped down on the nearest beanbag and took it from her. She skimmed through an introduction where the author was trying to prove she was cool, a bunch of statistics that proved the author was not cool, and a chapter titled "You're Awesome All by Yourself." The title of chapter three was "You Are Too Fierce for This." It was a list of mistakes people make. She read the headings: *Don't say you're fine when you're not. Don't be suspicious. Don't be a mind reader. Don't try to force someone to say, "I love you." Don't give ultimatums.* She looked up. "What's an ultimatum?"

Nina shrugged. "We'll figure it out. The point is— you're going to do *everything* this chapter says not to do. It's basically an instruction manual for how to get someone to dump you."

Eve glanced back down at the book. Some of those things sounded pretty sketchy. That's probably how they ended up on a DO NOT DO list. Is this the person she really wanted to be? She could feel Nina's eyes on her, waiting for her to respond.

Her phone dinged, and Eve dug it out of her pocket, grateful for a reason to stall for a few more seconds. It was from Andrew.

Lil Drummer Boi

> **What do you call a waffle that drinks too much Sprite?**

Eve rolled her eyes and was about to put the phone away when another message popped up.

Lil Drummer Boi

> **A belchin waffle**

Now she was mad. As if the stunt Andrew pulled on the way home yesterday wasn't bad enough, now he was sending her stupid jokes to remind her of it. What was his actual problem? Her hands tightened on the book. She could almost hear Sir Isaac Newton saying, "Every action has an equal and opposite reaction."

This had to happen. It was an immutable law of the universe.

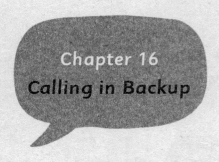

Chapter 16
Calling in Backup

At first, Andrew was a little worried about Eve not texting him back after the waffle joke. He'd been hoping for a *let's just be friends* text. When that didn't happen, he thought she'd at least send an emoji or whatever—something to prove that the weirdness from last week was all forgiven and they could go back to normal. But the drumline performed four times—twice on Saturday and twice on Sunday—at the town Harvest Festival. So mostly he was too busy drumming to think about it.

Despite Eve's radio silence, Andrew jumped out of bed on Monday morning ready to take anything life had to throw at him. While he waited for his waffles to toast, he told his mom about the huge crowd that had stopped to listen to their second set on Sunday. "They were cheering so loud for us. And it wasn't even like they had to. It wasn't just our parents like at band concerts."

"Dude, switch to decaf," Tom said through a mouthful of shredded wheat.

"Lay off him, Tom," Mom chided, taking a sip of not-decaf. "It's just a little residual adrenaline."

Andrew didn't mind Tom's ribbing today, though. He pounded "Uptown Funk" on the counter, catching a waffle as it popped up right on the cymbal crash part.

After downing six toaster waffles, Andrew put on extra deodorant, used some of Tom's Lucky cologne, and pulled on his second-favorite hoodie. While he brushed his teeth, he wondered if Eve would give his marching band hoodie back today. Even though she hadn't exactly said (or texted) the words, he was sure that, when she stormed off on Friday, that was the end of it. Today they could get back to normal.

So when his mom called up the stairs, "Andrew! Eve is here!" he didn't panic. He came down the stairs ready for a bone-popping hug and a look that agreed to pretend the whole thing never happened. He knew that hug and that look. That was how they made up two days after he accidentally broke her LEGO Mars rover. And the time she kicked him in the face doing flips in the pool. And probably twenty other times. They always found their way back.

"Hi, Eve!" he said. He was glad he was wearing the cologne. She'd probably say he smelled good when she hugged him.

"Hi. I thought we could walk to school together."

It was still the fake voice—high and silly. Only now Andrew thought it also sounded kind of pouty. Like when they were little, and their moms wouldn't give them cookies or whatever. A chill went through him.

His mom handed him a lunch bag. "Have a great day! Love you!"

He took the bag and his backpack and headed out the door with Eve, a vague sense of dread chipping away at his mood. Where was his "that never happened" hug? And why was she still doing *the voice*?

Eve was quiet, and at first Andrew thought maybe he was making a big deal about nothing. But then he noticed that she kept sighing and sniffling. Like crying but not crying. He ventured, "Are you okay?"

"I'm fine," she said in the least fine tone ever.

He tried again. "What's wrong?"

"Nothing." She said with another deep and sorrowful sigh.

Andrew was starting to worry for real. He said, "Did something happen with your parents?"

"I don't want to talk about it!" Eve practically yelled.

Ooooo-kay. Andrew decided to stop talking.

After a few minutes of silence interrupted only by Eve's sighing, she said, "What are you thinking about?"

He'd been thinking *BAH, DUH, BAH, bah, duh, duh, BAH, duh.* . . . He didn't know how to put mental drumming into words, so he said, "Nothing."

"You weren't thinking *nothing*," Eve proclaimed. "That's not possible."

Andrew shrugged.

"Why don't you want to tell me what you're thinking?" Eve asked, as if he must be committing thought crimes against humanity.

They were approaching the school now. Just a few more minutes and he'd be free. Ish.

Eve kept pushing. "Were you thinking about other girls?"

"What?"

"Oh my gosh! You were," Eve screeched.

"No, I wasn't," Andrew said, mostly confused and kind of irritated. He raised a hand to greet Arav and Jamal, who were getting out of Jamal's mom's minivan.

Eve took him by the shoulders, squaring up with him and talking loudly enough for everyone to hear. "Andrew . . . I mean *Andy*, I am your *girlfriend*. If you're too immature to handle that, then just tell me you want to break up."

I want to break up, thought Andrew. Arav and Jamal were giving him nods that said, *Do it*. But Holden had joined them and was looking too eager—the way Tom ogled Andrew's fries when he was hoping to eat whatever Andrew couldn't finish.

Andrew straightened up and set his jaw. *Not today, Holden.*

Eve growled in frustration—the most honest sound he'd heard from her so far this morning—before saying, "See you at lunch." She whirled around and marched into the school.

Shaking his head, he joined the guys, and the four of them headed toward the band room. As soon as Holden split off toward the horns section, Jamal said, "So you gonna dump her or what?"

Andrew shrugged. He fist-bumped Ramirez and nodded toward Madison as they reached the percussion area. Madison immediately went back to rudiments on her practice pads, but Ramirez looked at all their faces and said, "What's up?"

Arav described the scene outside the school while Andrew slowly died inside.

"That's messed up," Ramirez said. "What is wrong with your girlfriend?"

"I don't—"

"What's wrong with *you*?" Jamal demanded. "Why are

you letting her mess with you? She treats you like garbage. And the name thing? Does she think you're, like, her little pet dog?"

Andrew scrubbed at his forehead. This whole thing was giving him a headache.

Arav didn't say anything, but he shook his head disapprovingly as he slid his drumsticks out of his backpack.

Ramirez crossed his arms. "Seriously, why don't you break up with her?"

Andrew slumped into a plastic chair and confessed, "Eve is a terrible girlfriend. I know."

"The worst," Ramirez agreed.

"Train wreck," Jamal added.

"But she's a great friend." Andrew scrubbed at his hair. "I thought if I did all the stuff she hates, like embarrassing her and stuff, that she'd break up with me, and we could go back to just being friends." He told them about the epic Taki burp on Friday.

"DUDE, Ozzie. If she didn't dump you after that, she is *never* gonna dump you," Jamal said.

Arav finally spoke up. "I agree. She must have it really bad for you to stick around after that."

"Who cares?" said Ramirez. "Dump her. Now. Before she ruins Halloween."

Andrew knew they weren't wrong. But he could also

hear Tom's voice in his head saying, *If you friendzone Eve, she will hate you forever.*

Andrew realized that this was more than he could handle on his own. "Guys," he said, "I want to stop dating Eve, but I don't want to break up with her. I need your help."

Jamal raised his hand. "I volunteer as tribute. I'll dump her for you right now."

Andrew shook his head. "I don't want her to be sad or get her feelings hurt. And I really do want to be friends with her again. That's why I need her to be the one to end it. I don't know what else to do to get her to dump me, though."

The guys considered this logic puzzle seriously for a moment. Arav was the first to speak. "You guys know Brendan?"

"Yeah?" said Ramirez.

"He said Nina Moreno broke up with him because she thought his friends were immature jerks."

Ramirez snorted. "She called the whole boys' basketball team immature jerks?"

Arav gave an affirmative head tilt.

Ramirez blew his lips out in a *plbf* of definite pride. "We're *way* more immature than them."

Andrew thought aloud, "So girls will actually break up with guys because of stuff their friends do? That doesn't even make sense."

"Guys," said Jamal, faking a cough, "I don't feel good. I think it's *jerk-itis* coming on." He fake-coughed again. "Oh man, it's pretty contagious."

He put his fist out, the one he'd been coughing on, looking from Ramirez to Arav to Andrew meaningfully.

The guys looked at each other, smiles slowly spreading across their faces, a silent agreement forming between them. Three more fists joined Jamal's in the circle.

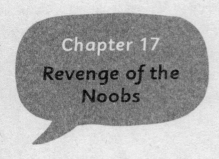

Chapter 17
Revenge of the Noobs

Eve peeked again at the book's rules for what not to do. During social studies, her last class before lunch, she already felt like garbage for how she'd acted this morning. Especially the "something's wrong, nothing's wrong" game. It felt too close to what her mom had done just before all the fighting.

She'd slam the dishes into the dishwasher. *What's wrong, Mom?* Nothing. She'd say, *You're finally home* when Dad walked in. *Did I do something wrong?* No, nothing. Then she'd make cutting comments under her breath about *that car*. It had gone on for months, until one day she'd stopped saying *Nothing's wrong* and started yelling.

Eve mentally scratched off *Give the silent treatment* from the book's list. That was one she couldn't do. It was *way* too close to home. But *Give ultimatums* seemed promising. She'd read that section over the weekend and found out that an ultimatum was a demand with consequences. Like when your parents say, *You'd better clean your room by Saturday, or we're taking your phone.* She could do that. She just needed to think of something she could hold over Andrew's head as the "or else."

"EVE," Mr. Wormlink said, tapping her desk with his pointer thing.

She snapped to attention. "What?"

"I asked you to name the states in New England."

"Um." Her cheeks got hot. "I thought New England *was* a state."

Only some people tried to muffle their laughter. Mr. Wormlink looked unamused. "Give me the book, Ms. McNeil."

She handed over the book, wishing she could turn invisible or sink through the floor.

Mr. Wormlink took it, making no effort to keep the class from seeing what it was. He said, "I advise you to spend more effort learning about this great land we live in and less effort chasing boys."

The class sniggered and *ooooe*d.

Please, thought Eve desperately, *just this once let a black hole open up right here.*

Mr. Wormlink cleared his throat, gave them all the death glare, and called on Reese to answer the question.

When the bell rang a thousand Mercury minutes later, Eve went straight for Mr. Wormlink's desk to try to get the book back. He couldn't just keep a library book. Could he? But half a dozen people were in her way, ribbing her about needing dating advice and how bad she was at geography. She had no choice but to abandon the book and duck out of the classroom.

But Reese dogged her every step, trying to be sympathetic. "Eve, it's totally understandable that you want to make things work with Andrew. He's a total cutie. But trust me, sometimes the worst thing you can do is try too hard. You know?"

"Yup. Right. See ya," Eve said, speeding away as fast as she could without risking getting a ticket for running in the hall.

She was one of the first people to get to the cafeteria and had to press through the crowd coming out. She sat at the girls' typical table and waited. Destiny showed up first. Then Jamal and Mateo. They shot her a curious look on their way past. Sofia came in with two other Cross Country girls and sat with them.

When Andrew and Arav came in, Eve jumped up and called, "ANDY! Over here! Sit with us!"

He froze, looking from his friends' table to her. Arav stared at her like she was a feral raccoon. Then Andrew took a step toward his friends.

Eve hurried to intercept him. It was ultimatum time. "Andy Wandy, come sit with us."

Andrew scratched his arm. "I, um, always sit with the guys."

Eve stomped her foot and crossed her arms. "I sat with you guys last week. It's your turn to sit with my friends. You have to sit with us or I'll . . ." Eve leaned in and cupped her hand over Andrew's ear. "I'll tell everyone your middle name is Annas."

As the words left her mouth, Eve felt a stab of guilt in the vicinity of her heart. Junior high is no place to expose that kind of weakness.

Andrew looked at her with horror in his eyes. Like he just realized she was a practicing cannibal. Eve held his gaze, battling back the instinct to beg forgiveness.

After an awkward pause, Andrew said, "Are you—?"

He shook his head, shot one more look at his friends' table, and then made a pleading face toward Arav. With a firm nod, Arav strode away like a man on a mission. Then Andrew plodded toward the girls, watching his feet the whole way.

Eve felt worse with every step. That was *too* mean. She should have pulled the punch. Why didn't she think of something else for the ultimatum? Why did she check out that terrible book in the first place? She never should have listened to Nina.

But now it was too late. Andrew was sitting next to Sofia, and there was nothing to do but go sit on the other side of him. Maybe she could make up for the ultimatum by being nice to him for the rest of the day.

Andrew didn't even glance at her when she sat down. She nudged him, but he refused to look up from his leftover casserole.

Eve said, "That smells good. Your mom makes the best chicken-broccoli casserole."

Andrew didn't respond.

The girls were obviously picking up on the tension. Their typically loud conversation had gone quiet. Eve poked at her taco salad.

Suddenly the table was invaded. Jamal, Mateo, and Arav swooped in and sat down, elbowing girls out of the way to make room. Eve thought she saw Andrew give the guys a grateful look, which she couldn't blame him for.

"Oh, hi guys," Destiny said. She gave Eve a look like *What's going on?* Eve shrugged.

Jamal took a huge bite of his sandwich before answering with his mouth full, "Just figured we'd hang with you guys today." At least, Eve *thought* that's what he said. It was hard to know for sure with so much food in his mouth. He proceeded to chew loudly and then, before swallowing, opened his mouth as wide as it would go.

The girls all visibly leaned away, noses crinkling and mouths puckered. Mateo called, "See food!" And all the guys laughed. Arav snorted. Andrew leaned over the table and high-fived Jamal like it was the best joke in the world.

Eve gagged on her salad.

From that point on, it seemed to be a competition for who could be the grossest. They made noises Eve didn't even know it was possible to make, talked about pooping, and ate like literal animals. Mateo sucked Jell-O out of a cup without using a spoon and then squirted it through the gap between his front teeth. Arav described in gruesome detail how hot dogs are made. All three of them reenacted a video game with copious explosions. Every time some imaginary target blew up, the whole table got sprayed with a fine mist of boy spit.

Eve pushed her food away. She probably wouldn't be able to eat for *days*. She caught the other girls' eyes and mouthed, *Sorry*, because she felt personally responsible for bringing this scourge upon them. Every one of them looked like they might vomit.

Suddenly Jamal stood, pressed his butt against Mateo's side, and said, "Tag! You're it!"

"HA HA! Fart tag! It is SO on!" Mateo said.

Andrew had a coughing fit.

"Wait," Destiny said. "Did he just *fart* on you?"

The boys couldn't answer because they were all laughing so hard.

The bell rang, and all the girls practically dived away from the table. Eve couldn't get out of the cafeteria fast enough. Literally. Because of the traffic jam at the doors, she couldn't escape. The next thing she knew, Andrew and Mateo were jostling each other right up against her, and Mateo was laughing, "You're it!"

When she finally made it through the doors, she took off, completely not caring if she got a ticket for running.

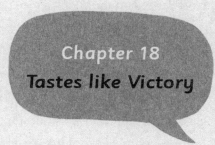

Chapter 18
Tastes like Victory

The guys were still juiced from their victory at lunch when they got to band last period. Jamal had tears rolling down his cheeks from laughing so hard as he told them, "Girl saw me in the hall and just took off running."

Clutching his sore abs, Andrew said, "Dude, how did you think of fart tag on the fly like that?"

Ramirez slapped Andrew on the back. "Oz, you're a free man. She's for sure gonna dump you now."

"I'm surprised she didn't do it already," Arav said. "Hasn't she texted you yet?"

Andrew shrugged. "My phone is off. Doesn't anybody else follow the school rules?"

The guys all looked at him like he was weird. *Okay,* thought Andrew, *just me.*

"My phone's off," Madison offered from where she sat cross-legged on the floor.

Andrew looked at her in surprise. With her rebellious rock-star look, she could be voted "least likely to follow the rules." But also, he didn't think she ever listened to their conversations. She was always so aloof. He cleared his throat and gave her an appreciative smile. Her lips tightened into not-quite-a-smile. He couldn't be sure, but he thought maybe they understood each other.

"Drumline, bring it in!" Mr. Handen called over the din of warm-ups. He walked toward them, waving an arm for them to huddle up.

Madison stood and brushed off her black jeans. The guys formed a loose circle and went to parade rest out of habit—feet apart, shoulders back, chests out, chins up, sticks together in both hands.

Mr. Handen chuckled, "At ease, gentlemen."

Madison cleared her throat loudly.

Mr. Handen nodded toward her. "And lady."

They all went back to slouching.

"Before we start practice today, we have a little business to take care of," Mr. Handen announced. "As you may have noticed, there's a nip in the air. That means marching season is drawing to a close. Next week we start learning concert music."

There was a collective groan from the whole percussion section. Andrew probably groaned loudest of all. Concert season was dead boring. Standing around for half a song so you can ding a triangle or something. He hated it. Marching season was *everything*.

Mr. Handen held up a hand to quiet them. "I know, guys. That's why I told them that the drumline *would* be interested in playing at Glow Night in three weeks."

Andrew's emphatic yes blended with yeses from the guys around him. He didn't know what he was agreeing to, but Mr. Handen had him at "playing."

Madison's and Arav's hands shot into the air.

"Yes, Madison?" Mr. Handen said, when the cheering had quieted down.

"Who's organizing this?" Madison asked.

"Well, Ms. Medgar is the faculty advisor. There are several students from the Events Committee of Student Council helping put it together. And they've enlisted us, the art classes, and the A/V club to help out. So it's going to be a team effort."

"Will we be learning new cadences?" Madison asked. Arav, whose hand was still in the air, gave her a peeved look.

"We'll do the ones we know—school fight song,

'Uptown Funk,' 'Blastoff,' and 'Good Times.' And—if you guys are up for it—we could work on a new one too."

"YEAH!" the whole group cheered.

"Where is it?" Madison asked, apparently believing that getting called on gave her the floor indefinitely.

"Here. In the gym." Mr. Handen nodded to Arav, finally acknowledging his raised hand. "Arav?"

"What exactly is a Glow Night? Is it like a dance?"

A few people laughed like that was a dumb question. But Andrew had been secretly wondering the same thing.

Mr. Handen crossed his arms and looked professorly. "It's more like a glow-in-the-dark party. They're going to set up black lights in the gym and decorate everything neon."

"That sounds awesome!" Ramirez called out.

"Can we decorate our drums?" Andrew asked, forgetting to raise his hand.

"What do you have in mind?"

Everyone started talking at once. They could paint their drumsticks, use gaffer's tape, drum with glow sticks, paint their whole bodies like Blue Man Group. Then it turned into an argument about whether Blue Man Group was really painted or wearing skins and whether or not they would have to get new drums for every performance because of all the paint.

"Okay, guys," Mr. Handen interrupted. "You've got a few

weeks to figure all that out. For now, mark your calendars for the first Saturday in November and plan on some extra practices between now and then."

Mr. Handen went to the podium at the front of the room to call the band to order. Andrew smiled for the rest of band class.

An hour later, he popped in a piece of mint gum while he took his place in parade formation for after-school practice. It tasted like he felt—cool and confident. Thanks to his friends, he'd definitely won the war with Eve. Glow Night was going to be amazing. And concert season had just gotten shortened by three weeks. Everything was going his way.

When he caught a disgusted look from Eve as she ran past with the Cross Country team, he smiled bigger than ever. The only thing that could make this day more epic would be the text from her saying, *I want to break up. We're better as friends.*

Once they were friends again, he would tell her all about Glow Night and they could spend the next three weeks planning together how to make it even more awesome. Eve always had great ideas for stuff like that.

But that text never came.

Chapter 19
I'm the Problem. It's Me.

Eve slammed the door and threw her backpack onto the floor. Her skin was still crawling from "see food" and "fart tag." She'd gotten two tickets for running in the hall trying to stay away from those guys this afternoon, terrified that they would pause near her and announce, "You're it." She honestly didn't think she could survive that.

The only good thing about the boys' repulsive disgustingness was that it made her feel better about her own behavior. Ever since she'd checked out that book, she'd been feeling guilty. But now she felt like, in comparison to how Andrew and his friends acted, her behavior was totally acceptable.

"What's wrong?" her mom asked, emerging from the kitchen. "I heard the door slam."

Eve automatically took stock of the situation. Her mom looked calm except for the now-permanent frown lines around her eyes and mouth. There was no smell of food cooking. Her dad's Dodge Charger wasn't in the driveway, so she figured he wasn't home from work yet.

Her policy was to always tell her mom that things were going great with Andrew. So the answer to *What's wrong?* should absolutely be *Nothing!* She tried to work up the lie.

"You look like you just stepped in poop or something," Mom said.

Dang, she was *good*. Mom had just summed up her day perfectly.

Eve let out a deep breath. "Why are guys so gross?"

Her mom's mouth quirked up a little. It was almost a smile. Eve found herself telling her the whole story, making sure to put all the blame on general "guys" and not say anything bad about Andrew. Mom looked very serious as she listened—almost too serious.

When Eve finished, Mom said soberly, "Do you feel safe?"

"What?" Eve pulled a face. "Mom, they're not scary. They're just dumpster-dwelling turd brains."

Mom burst out laughing. "Oh," she gasped, holding her ribs. "Wow."

Eve huffed, "What?! They are! They're nasty gross."

133

"This from the girl who just said 'dumpster-dwelling turd brains.'" Mom shrugged. "They're junior high boys."

"Seriously, Mom? Are you going to say 'boys will be boys'? Because I can't with that."

Mom raised an eyebrow. "It's not like girls are sweet angels. Hon, you are *gross*. I've stopped counting how many pairs of sweaty socks you've left around this house. And your bathroom looks like a troll cave." Before Eve had time to get offended, Mom put her arm around her. "And I love you. And if you need me to, you know I'll go Mama Bear in a *second*."

"Please don't," Eve said, horrified. Having her mom storm the school, claws out, would definitely result in death-inducing humiliation.

Eve realized she couldn't remember the last time her mom had been completely focused on *her*. It felt really good. She put her head on her mom's shoulder and admitted, "I guess you're right."

Mom laughed again. "The rarest words from a teenager's mouth! I'm flattered." She gave Eve a squeeze-and-jiggle. "Try to have a little grace for those guys. Nobody's done growing up yet."

Eve nodded, not sure what "a little grace" would look like in real life. She was *not* letting anyone fart on her. And she never wanted to eat within ten feet of them again. Speaking of eating, she needed food. She'd been too nauseated for lunch, and now she was starving. "What's for dinner?" she asked.

"I was thinking about ordering Chinese. What do you think?"

Alarm bells blared in Eve's head: *Warning. Maximum payload exceeded.* This was something different. They never ordered out on weeknights. "Where's Dad?" she asked, afraid of the answer.

Mom averted her eyes, but Eve could see the tightness all around her mouth. Her words sounded clipped when she said, "Working late. Just us tonight."

Eve didn't know if it was true. And she didn't know if her mom knew if it was true. Was this her mom's cover story for her dad? Or her dad's cover story for why he didn't come home? Or maybe he really was working late. All Eve knew for sure was that she wanted her dad to come home. And, like, *be* home. She wanted them to eat all together around the table like they used to. She wanted her parents to talk to each other. She wanted to not always be wondering if her life was about to crash to the earth in a raging fireball.

Food didn't sound good after all.

Mom made a quick conversational lane change. "How's Andrew? Is he one of the guys on the naughty list for the bad behavior today?"

Eve knew her mom was changing the subject to keep Eve from asking questions about Dad. That's what the topic of Andrew had become for them—something safe to talk about so they didn't have to face the thing with fangs and claws that lurked behind closed doors and between the lines of every conversation. The monster that was tearing their family apart.

At the same moment, Eve also realized that avoiding the monster was exactly what she wanted to do too. And talking to her mom about a problem with Andrew would work better than saying everything was fine. So she said, "Um, kind of? I don't know what to do about him."

"Okay. I'm gonna order some food, and then I want you to tell me all about it."

Over sesame chicken and egg rolls, Mom said, "So. Why don't you know what to do about Andrew?"

This was tricky. Eve needed to give her mom enough information to keep them both focused on this. But she had to be careful not to be too honest and get herself in trouble. Cautiously she admitted, "I guess I don't always know how to act as a girlfriend."

"Well, it's your first time. Do you think Andrew's maybe feeling the same way?"

"Yeah, maybe. I hadn't really thought about it."

Mom popped a mushroom into her mouth. "He's a really sweet boy."

Eve harrumphed and shoveled in a clump of rice. He *could be* sweet. Or he could burp in your face and force-feed you pudding. Then again, he wasn't the one giving ultimatums and literally making stuff up to be upset about. Her face burned at the memory of how she'd been acting. She hadn't told her mom about any of that. And she wasn't going to.

"Relationships take work," Mom said with a sigh. "And sometimes you have to decide whether the return is worth the investment."

"What?" Eve was scared they weren't talking about Andrew anymore.

"You have to decide if what you're getting out of the relationship is worth the work you're putting into it," Mom explained. "Self-love also means knowing when to walk away."

Now Eve was practically positive they weren't talking about Andrew. How could her mom say that? Was she basically coming right out and telling her she was going to divorce her dad? Why couldn't they just figure their stuff out and act like grown-ups?

Panicking, Eve blurted, "And sometimes you just need to try harder! Because breaking up isn't an option, and you realize *you're* the one making it terrible!"

"Eve?" Mom set her chopsticks down, both eyebrows up.

Eve stood, shoving her chair back with a clatter. "We're not breaking up! *Nobody* is breaking up!" Then she ran up to her room, slammed the door, and threw herself onto her bed.

She lay there fuming. Why couldn't Mom just be nicer to Dad? She was the one being impossible to live with and driving him away. He probably didn't come home tonight because he knew she'd just pick a fight. And now she had the nerve to say that she wasn't "getting enough" for what she was "putting into it"? As far as Eve could see, she wasn't putting *anything* into it except accusations and ultimatums.

And then somehow Eve was hearing herself demanding, *Were you thinking about other girls? I'll tell everyone your middle name. I am your girlfriend. If you're too immature to handle that, then just tell me you want to break up. . . . What are you thinking about?* The whole day, every nasty thing she'd said, replayed on a loop.

She wanted to be mad at her mom, at Andrew, at *somebody*. But the person she was really mad at was herself. The ultimatum, the accusations, the yelling. She sounded like her mom—the worst version of her mom. How could Andrew not hate her? Maybe he did.

When she couldn't take the guilt anymore, she got out her phone to text Andrew.

> Sorry for all the stuff I said
> today

But then she didn't hit send. It just felt like not enough.

If she really wanted Andrew to forgive her, she should go over and apologize for real. And then maybe he'd ask about her parents, and this time she'd tell him everything.

Eve rang the bell at Andrew's house and waited, knees bouncing. She was stuck in Mercury time again—the seconds ticking by in slow motion. It was already dark, even though it was just after seven thirty. Her dad still wasn't home yet. She hadn't told her mom that she was leaving. It was getting cold, and she hadn't grabbed a coat.

And she wasn't sure if she was welcome here anymore.

Just as Eve was about to cut her losses and run, Andrew opened the door. The smell of chocolate wafted out on the warm air from inside the house. It was rich and welcoming and somehow made Eve feel even more like an astronaut with no tether—adrift and alone.

Andrew looked at her suspiciously. "What?"

Eve had a speech all planned out, explaining everything and how sorry she was and that she didn't want to lose Andrew as a friend. But all that came out was, "I just . . . I,

139

um." And then suddenly her throat was too tight and her eyes were burning. She looked away, swiping at her face. Determined not to let Andrew see her fall apart.

"Eve? Sweetie?" Mrs. Ozdemir edged Andrew out of the way and, without asking any questions, pulled Eve into the house and into a tight hug. "I'm glad you're here. You don't need to explain anything if you don't want to."

This hug felt so safe and secure. Eve felt herself relaxing for the first time all day.

After a minute, Mrs. Ozdemir held her at arm's length and said, "I've got brownies in the oven. You want to stay for a while?"

The urge to cry receded. Eve nodded, still not completely trusting herself to try talking again.

"Come on," Mrs. Ozdemir said, shepherding her into the kitchen with Andrew trailing behind. "I'll text your mom that you're here."

Eve silently scoffed that her mom didn't deserve the courtesy. But Mom and Mrs. O were best friends, so Eve kept her bitter thoughts to herself.

Without looking at her, Andrew plunked himself at the kitchen table, where his math homework was already in progress. The sight of the open math book gave Eve a twinge of guilt.

"I haven't even started algebra," she admitted.

For a Mercury second, Andrew stared silently at his paper. Finally he said, "You can look off my book if you want."

Eve took the seat next to him, accepted the sheet of graph paper and pencil he offered her, and started on the first problem. She smiled to herself while she multiplied polynomials, feeling like Andrew had given her more than school supplies. He was offering her a tether—a way back to how it used to be. No awkward conversations or big apologies necessary. They could pretend none of the garbage and weirdness had ever happened.

She breathed a sigh of relief.

Chapter 20
Variables and Other Mysteries

Andrew hated variables. Your whole life, you do math with numbers, and then suddenly they start saying, *Now solve a way harder problem, and also you don't get to know what the numbers are.* Why couldn't someone just tell him what he was dealing with?

Like, why did Eve come over here? Could she smell the brownies baking from across the street? And why did his mom act like Eve was a refugee or something? *You don't need to explain anything*, she'd said, even though Andrew wished Eve would explain about twenty things. He wasn't oblivious—he could tell she was upset about something. But if he asked her what was wrong, she'd just say, *Nothing*.

Eve sitting next to him doing algebra right now made about as much sense as $f(x) = -1/x$

He slapped his pencil onto the table. "When are we ever going to use this in real life?"

Eve made a noise of agreement. "Right?"

Andrew leaned back in his chair. "I mean, maybe *you* will when you're, like, measuring the atmospheric pressure on Jupiter or something."

Eve turned and offered him a smile. Not the fake one—a real one. His heart did a triplet. He'd really missed that smile.

"Which one are you mad at?" she asked.

He almost said, *I'm NOT mad. Just tell me what's going on.* But instead he mumbled, "Number seven." Because even algebra was easier to figure out than eighth-grade relationships.

Eve leaned over and looked at his paper. Then she said, "You almost have it. Just remember, you aren't solving for *f*. You're solving for the function of *x*. You're making it harder than it really needs to be."

"What's a function?"

Eve shrugged. "Honestly? I have no idea. I just plug in the numbers."

Andrew had to laugh. It was kind of nice to know that Eve didn't have *everything* figured out. He leaned over his paper again. Eve's hair smelled like strawberry candy, which made it hard to force his eyes to focus on equations for some reason.

Then a plate of brownies landed in front of them, and his mom sang, "Brain break," before disappearing again.

Eve dived onto the plate and took a huge bite of brownie, closing her eyes while she chewed. Andrew watched her, mesmerized by the chocolate on her lips and the yummy noises she was making.

A sharp blow to the back of his head snapped him out of it. Andrew went, *"Ow."*

Tom scooped up three brownies in one hand and used the other to clobber Andrew again. This time Andrew was ready for it and ducked his head to absorb the blow.

Tom made a quick getaway with his brownies before Andrew could strike back. Eve called after him, "Rude much?!" Then she reached over and tousled Andrew's hair on the spot Tom had clipped him.

Andrew's heart did a five stroke roll. It occurred to him that if Eve didn't want to tell him why she'd been acting so off, it was okay. He didn't need to know. They didn't have to say the breakup words or figure anything out, as long as it could be like this now.

He wasn't going to make it harder than it needed to be.

"Here." Eve put a brownie into his hand. "Brownies make everything better."

The next half hour was easy. They laughed and talked just like they used to. Except it wasn't exactly like before, because now they were boyfriend and girlfriend. For the first time, that actually felt like a good thing. A *really* good thing.

They eventually solved all the functions, simplified all the equations, and ate all the brownies. When his mom called from the living room that it was getting late on a school night, Andrew said, "I'll walk you home."

Eve laughed. "It's like fourteen steps away."

Andrew shrugged. "I know." Now that things were good again, he was determined to hold on to every possible moment. He opened the door for her, which she didn't seem to mind this time. He waited for her to step past him before closing the door and catching up with her.

As they crossed the street, Andrew said, "I'm glad you came over."

He was pretty proud of himself for stringing that many words together. Because mostly he was imagining holding her hand.

"Me too," she said. Her hand was in a fist at her side.

Would she jerk away if he took it, like she did at the dance? Or would it be different, like holding the door was, now that they were alone? He wanted to try it and find out. Or maybe he was supposed to ask before touching. Is that how it worked?

A cold breeze blew a few stray leaves past their feet. Eve shivered and hugged herself, and Andrew realized neither of them had a coat on.

"Do you need me to keep you warm?" he offered, feeling like even Tom would think that was pretty smooth. But Eve just laughed again.

So, asking was *not* how it worked. Or maybe there was more than one way to ask.

"Eve—" He put a hand on her arm as they reached the sidewalk. And she didn't bolt. She turned toward him, looking maybe a little puzzled, but not disgusted. It felt like a yes.

His heart accelerated to about two hundred beats per minute. He stepped in closer, sliding his other arm around her, pulling her a little closer. She didn't resist.

The cold wind had painted pink across her cheeks and nose. Her eyes were open wide. Tendrils of hair had escaped from her ponytail. They fluttered across her forehead and along her cheeks. He didn't think she was breathing. He knew he wasn't.

If he kissed her, he wondered, would it taste like brownies? Would she kiss him back?

They were standing at the edge of the illuminated circle from the streetlight. He took a step forward, still holding her, moving them both into the shadow. She followed his lead, never taking her eyes off him. Sliding her hand up his arm. It felt like a dance.

And then the porch light snapped on.

Eve jumped away from him like she'd been electrocuted.

She looked frantically at the house and back at him, blurted, "Good night," and ran.

Andrew stood on the street looking at the house long after the door closed behind her. He stood there so long that eventually the motion detector on the porch light decided he was a bush or something and clicked back off.

After barely sleeping, Andrew got up early the next day and got ready. He tried extra hard to make his hair look cool and his breath minty fresh. He even used his dad's mouthwash, which burned so much, it made his eyes water. When he couldn't wait anymore, he went back to Eve's house to ask her to walk to school with him.

He felt invincible. This was *his* day. He owned this day. Sure, things hadn't gone exactly as he'd pictured them last night, but right before she'd freaked out, she'd said yes to him a dozen ways. And before that . . . before that they'd had fun, and she'd been kind and real—like her old self. He'd played it back a thousand times in his head, and it got sweeter every time.

Now that he knew what it could really be like to be Eve McNeil's boyfriend, he was all in.

"Good morning, Andrew," Eve's mom said at the door. Somehow it sounded like an apology. "Eve's not feeling a hundred percent this morning. She might go in to school a little later."

"Is she okay?" he asked, feeling himself deflating. "Is she sick?"

"She's fine. Just not feeling great."

Andrew texted Eve while he walked to school.

hope you feel better

After a few seconds, Eve gave his text a thumbs-up. That was it.

He spent the whole walk to school wondering what the heck was going on. If Eve was "fine," she'd come to school. If she were sick, she'd stay home, not come "later." But she wasn't sick at all last night. Was she avoiding him? Did she tell her mom to lie to him? Did he completely misunderstand what had happened last night?

Andrew was concentrating so hard on all the new variables that he didn't notice that Madison was in the band room until she chucked a maraca at him.

"Hey!" he protested.

"Hey yourself, space cadet." Madison looked him over and made a face like he'd failed a test.

"Why are you here so early?" Andrew asked, only slightly caring. What he really wanted to ask her was why a girl would seem like she wanted to kiss you and then ten hours later have her mom bounce you.

"I wanted to get in some extra practice on the new cadence," Madison said, "and my parents forbid me to drum from eight p.m. to ten a.m., so I have to come here." It was officially the most words she had ever said to him at one time.

Maybe *all* girls were cold to you one day and Chatty Cathy the next. Or maybe he just didn't understand the rules. Madison was probably right, and he really was a noob.

Why couldn't things stay simple? When you were a kid, the rules were *simple*. Look both ways before crossing the street. Don't touch broken glass. Obey your parents. Tell the truth. Now everything was mixed up, and figuring out the rules was like trying to drum in some weird time signature. Like you're drumming along in four-four to "Here Comes the Sun" and then *bam*, you hit the bridge and all of a sudden it's in eleven-eight time.

" . . . because that would be too messy, so I think we should wear black T-shirts and jeans."

Andrew realized Madison had been talking to him and was now looking at him expectantly for a response. He said, "Uh . . . okay."

Madison rolled her eyes and made a sound that clearly meant *Why do I bother*.

Andrew's cheeks went hot. "Sorry. I guess I'm not used to you talking to me."

"Why would I," said Madison, "when you guys act like I'm an alien or something."

"No," Andrew protested, "*you* act like *we're* all weirdos."

"You are." She grinned. "But who else am I going to be friends with?"

Andrew threw the maraca back at her.

"Hey!" Madison jabbed him with her mallet. Andrew parried, and they ended up in a full-on sword fight with their mallets, which was extra fun because of all the lectures they'd gotten about only using drumsticks for drumming. It was a welcome break from obsessing over Eve's mystifying behavior.

Midfight, Madison suddenly stopped swinging her mallet and said, "Oh, hey, Jamal."

Jamal was giving Andrew a look—half accusation, half admiration.

Andrew said, "What?"

Arav and Ramirez walked in. Ramirez was saying, " . . . only two more weeks till Halloween! It is gonna be *so* epic this year. Right?"

Arav said, "Yeah!"

Madison turned away and went back to pounding on the practice pads.

For the first time, Andrew saw the move for what it

was—self-defense. She thought they didn't want her around. But Madison had come right out and said she wanted to be friends with them. Compared to the unsolvable Eve puzzle, this felt like a no-brainer.

Before he could overthink it, he blurted, "Madison, do you want to trick-or-treat with us?"

The guys gaped at him.

Madison's mallets went still for a second. Then she shrugged. "Probably." She started drumming again.

Arav pointed and mouthed, *You and her?*

Jamal nodded with his whole upper body.

Andrew shook his head.

"Aaaaanyway," Ramirez continued, dropping his backpack at his feet. "I guess you and Eve broke up."

"Uh . . ." Andrew tried to think of a way to summarize the highs and lows of the past twelve hours. All he came up with was, "Nope."

Ramirez looked from Andrew to Madison—who was determinedly looking only at her music—and said, "I don't get it."

Jamal chuckled, pulling his drumsticks out of his backpack before dropping the bag by the wall.

Andrew scratched his head. First Eve ghosted him this morning, and now somehow everyone had the wrong idea about him and Madison. Was he just bad at life?

Ramirez rubbed his hands together. "Okay, well, I've got an awesomely immature idea." He looked very proud of himself. "Friday night, we fork her yard!"

"I'm in!" Holden called, appearing in the doorway. "Whose yard?"

"Eve's! It would be hilarious! Plus, we've got to get Andrew free by Halloween."

"No," Andrew said, at the same moment Jamal said, "Nah."

"WHAT?!" Ramirez looked at them like they'd broken the bro code—another set of rules Andrew was pretty sure he didn't understand.

"I'm back together with Reese," Jamal said casually. "She'd probably be salty about it."

Andrew said, "And I don't want Eve to break up with me anymore."

"WHAT?!" Ramirez said again. "We agreed! You have to get dumped! Your girlfriend is the worst. She's gonna ruin Halloween!"

"No, she's not," Andrew insisted. "She's just . . . I don't know—"

Before Andrew could come up with a way to explain about Eve, the five-minute bell rang. Everyone hoisted their backpacks and went to their first-hour classes.

Chapter 21
If It's Not Me, It's Not Anyone

"You are NOT going to believe this!" Destiny roared as she burst through the cafeteria door.

Nina, who was on Student Council, had roped half the Cross Country team into staying after school to paint backdrops for Glow Night. So now here they were in the cafeteria, surrounded by neon paints and white sheets. And, thanks to Destiny's dramatic entrance, all of them were now waiting to hear something unbelievable.

Destiny marched straight to where Nina and Eve were kneeling on the floor next to a neon-orange paint bucket. Then she planted her feet, put her hands on her hips, and practically shouted to the room, "Andrew is cheating on Eve!"

"No," Eve said without hesitation. She knew Andrew. He was not that guy. Especially after last night, there was no way.

Before last night, their relationship had been such a disaster that she might have believed anything. But then he'd offered her that tether. He didn't make her explain or grovel. They were friends again.

More than friends.

The memory of standing so close to him in the dark sent a shiver up her spine. She'd almost kissed him. Until the stinking light had come on and she'd panicked, it had been magical.

Before, she'd tried to imagine kissing people—Jamal, Mateo, Brendan, Holden, even Sofia and Nina—and just gotten grossed out. She honestly didn't get what the big deal was. Until last night.

The scene ran through her mind again, half memory, half fantasy. Andrew looking at her like she was a mystery of the universe. Sliding his hand around her waist. Pulling her closer as her eyes fluttered closed—

"He IS," Destiny insisted. "Everyone is talking about it. Him and Madison got caught, like, making out in the band room this morning."

"NO WAY!" Nina said, but it sounded like *tell me all about it.*

This can't be happening, Eve thought.

"It must be a mistake," Sofia said.

Reese approached with her paintbrush held high, dripping hot pink speckles onto the floor. "It's true. Maybe not making out, but definitely flirting hard-core. Jamal told me."

Nina cocked her head at Reese. "Didn't you guys break up?"

"We got back together," Reese said with a sly smile. "The point is, Andrew definitely has something going on with Madison."

Eve was in shock. Her brain was rebooting again. And then Nina was pulling her away from the group and whisper-yelling, "This could be a good thing! This is great. Like, ick, gross. Not great. But, like, you *wanted* him to break up with you, so."

Sofia closed the space that Nina had created. "This is sooooo terrible. There must be some explanation," she moaned. "I just don't think he would do that. Plus you guys are literally sooo perfect together."

Nina shrugged. "Sofia, not every couple is Romeo and Juliet."

"They both died," Destiny interjected.

"Whatever," Nina said, undeterred. "What I'm saying is, we're like thirteen, and it's normal to shop around."

Sofia's mouth fell open.

Nina plowed on. "Hear me out. I like chocolate ice

cream. But I'm not going to get chocolate ice cream *every single time*. It gets boring. You want to try a fresh flavor."

Eve couldn't keep the horror off her face. What about true love? What about commitment? How could it be okay for someone—after *ten* years of being friends or, let's say, *seventeen* years of marriage—to just *want a fresh flavor*?

Was it really possible that, after almost kissing her last night, Andrew was already trying out a *fresh flavor*?

Sofia said, "I've *never* gotten tired of chocolate ice cream. That's not real."

Maybe it was because she'd panicked. He probably thought she didn't like him, so he'd moved on to someone who didn't act like a cat with a shock collar.

And then this morning she'd woken up with cramps—which honestly explained so much about how emotional she was yesterday—and didn't even come to school until fifth hour. She hadn't responded to his "hope you feel better" text because he'd just ask what was wrong. After repenting from playing the "nothing's wrong" game, she couldn't use that to dodge the question. And she'd rather die than tell a guy she was having her period. But now he probably thought she was ghosting him. Would he really have given up on her this easily?

Reese nodded sagely, saying, "You're not wrong, Nina. That's why they say relationships take work. You know?"

Eve felt like she was going to throw up. Her mom had said the exact same thing, right before that horrible *You have to decide if they're worth the investment.* Had Andrew decided she wasn't worth it? Had her parents decided that about their family? Maybe nobody thought she was worth sticking around for.

From about ten feet away, Reese said, "Plus, no offense, but Eve *was* pretty awful to him. You can't totally blame him."

Eve couldn't help but agree. She had literally been inventing new ways to be awful.

"I totally *can*," Destiny said. "There's no excuse for cheating." She picked up a paintbrush and added X eyes to a giant emoji face.

Eve agreed with that, too. How could Andrew do this to her?

"Destiny's right. He's a total skeeze. I literally hate him now," Nina said authoritatively. "But, also, there are plenty of fish in the sea. Just get back out there and sparkle, Eve."

Eve did not feel like fishing or sparkling. All she felt like doing was running away and crying.

"I'm just saying, what do you expect?" Reese said, and *tsk*ed.

"I expect to be treated like a queen. And so does Eve. Right, girl?"

"Well, sorry, but that's not real life. Relationships are

fifty-fifty, give and take. And, I'm the one with a boyfriend, so." She left it at that, letting the rest of them fill in the implied *Obviously I know what I'm talking about.*

Sofia sighed. "I wish I had a boyfriend. I wish Mark Chen would ask me out."

Nina huffed, "Just ask him out already."

Sofia wailed, "I *caaaan't.* What if he says no?!"

Reese swirled a heart onto the sheet. "I could ask Jamal to ask him if he likes you."

Sofia brightened. "Would you? But he wouldn't tell him that I told you to tell him to ask him, would he?"

Eve's brain couldn't begin to untangle that sentence.

Nina rolled her eyes at Eve. Eve pretended not to see and concentrated very hard on painting the solar system. Nina wasn't wrong that Sofia's unrelenting crush on Mark Chen was getting ridiculous. But it just felt wrong to roll your eyes at someone so sweet. Sofia never said anything mean ever. Not even to people who deserved it.

Reese set her brush in the paint tray and took out her phone. "I'll text him."

"Wait!" Sofia threw out her hands, creating a Jackson Pollock–style paint splat on the backdrop. "What if he doesn't like me?! That would be humiliating."

Reese paused and looked up. "Don't worry. I'll just tell Jamal to tell Mark that you *might* like him, *if* he likes you."

Eve slashed a mad face onto Jupiter with angry red paint. Her heart felt like it was cracking into pieces. For weeks, all she'd wanted was for Andrew to break up with her so that they could get back to being friends. But then last night was *better* than friends.

But now Andrew liked someone else.

Even from a distance Eve could tell that Madison was legit cool. She had chopped all her hair off and obviously didn't care what anybody thought about it. She wasn't just the only girl on drumline—she was captain. Plus, she wore combat boots with a Hello Kitty backpack. Eve couldn't help but admire her self-confidence.

But Madison wasn't the one who had cleaned bloody gravel out of Andrew's knee when he crashed his bike and his mom wasn't home, so she didn't know where he'd gotten that scar. She didn't sit up with him for hours because he was too scared to go to bed after his brother showed him that Chucky movie, so she didn't know to only let Andrew watch comedies. She couldn't know that he practiced every cadence for a hundred and twenty hours in his backyard until he got it perfect. Nobody but Eve knew how hard he worked when he really wanted something.

When Eve thought of Andrew sharing his mom's brownies with Madison, it made her stomach hurt. When she imagined him slo-mo fighting Madison, it felt like getting scissor-kicked for real. If he were dating Madison, then *she* would be the person he randomly texted and joked around with and gave rib-crushing hugs to. She would be the one who got the text **Can you come over? I'm positive there is a demon-possessed doll in my closet.**

Eve felt like something was being stolen from her.

Now that it was too late, she realized she wanted to be Andrew's person. It was *supposed* to be her. But she figured it out too late. She'd already lost him. She knew it with sickening certainty.

None of the girls seemed to notice Eve's meltdown in progress. Reese circled the conversation back to Nina's ice cream analogy. "If Jamal dumped me for a fresh flavor, I'd probably burn his house down."

Nina snort-laughed.

For once, Eve knew exactly what Reese meant. Maybe minus the arson.

"Andrew is *not* breaking up with me for Madison," Eve announced, surprised by her own fierceness. "It's me or nobody."

Nina clicked her tongue. Sofia's face was sympathetic. Reese looked like she was getting ready to give more dating advice.

Nina raised an eyebrow. "You're like a Taylor Swift–level diva. You know that?"

Eve crossed her arms defensively. She didn't actually want to be a diva. But the idea of Andrew dating someone else was too horrible. She couldn't let that happen. She'd rather he be alone forever than belong to someone who was not her. Yes, that was beyond selfish, and she felt like a jerk. But that didn't make it not true. Eve told herself she'd volunteer at an animal shelter or something to balance it out.

Half an hour later, Eve and the other girls passed the drumline on their way out of the school.

Part of her desperately wanted to eye-beg him not to give up on her.

Part of her wanted to yell, *Now hear this! Andrew is my boyfriend, so everybody back off!*

She wanted to explain about last night . . . about this whole year.

To ask him if it was true that he liked Madison.

But just thinking about it made her throat tight and her eyes burn. She knew that if she didn't take drastic action, she would humiliate herself by crying in front of Andrew. In front of his drumline crew. In front of the whole Glow Night prep team. All of them would think she was pathetic. A weakling. An easy target.

There. Was. No. Way.

She didn't look at him. Couldn't look at him. Instead,

she lifted her chin to make sure they could all see how much she was not hurting. She was strong and confident and absolutely *fine*.

"Eve?" Andrew called after her.

She pretended not to hear.

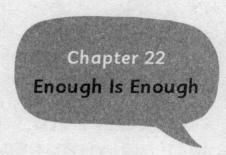

Chapter 22
Enough Is Enough

Andrew watched Eve leave for the second time in twenty-four hours without so much as glancing at him. He was *so sure* last night that she liked him back, and that all the crappiness was behind them. Now he wasn't sure about anything anymore.

A hand clapped on his shoulder, and Andrew forced his focus back to his crew. It was Jamal who was holding on to him. He said, "Hey, man, I got something."

"Huh?" Andrew noticed Jamal was holding a book.

Jamal turned it around so all the guys could see the front cover. It said *All the Tea: Talking, Dating, and True Love.* Jamal explained, "This was in Wormlink's room. Reese said Eve got caught reading it in class."

True love. It stuck in Andrew's brain. *True love.* For some reason those words brought back memories of Eve running toward him at the airport, throwing slo-mo punches in her purple dress, dancing with him in the dark—his heart pounding like the Blue Devils' drumline.

"A dating advice book?" Ramirez said, taking it from Jamal and fanning the pages. "I don't get it."

Andrew tried to make sense of it. Was Eve reading this because she wanted to be a better girlfriend? All he'd ever wanted was for her to be herself. But maybe something in this book was what brought her to his house last night. So that was okay.

Jamal looked like a movie cop with a lead. "There's a bookmark." He took it back from Ramirez, opened it to the saved page, and handed it to Andrew. Arav leaned over his drum, trying to get a better look.

Andrew read:

Chapter 3
You Are Too Fierce for This

They say love can drive you wild. And it sure can! Have you ever seen a totally nice, intelligent, otherwise well-adjusted human start dating someone and suddenly become as suspicious as a private eye, as selfish as a tod-dler with a new toy, and as hard to read as Old English?

Don't be that guy! In this chapter we're going to talk about the things people do that end up making people break up with them. Basically, we're going to talk about what not to do. Here's the short list:

- Don't say you're fine when you're not. There's a 99.9 percent chance you aren't dating a mind reader!
- Speaking of which, don't try to be a mind reader. You won't be very good at it.
- Don't be suspicious. Nobody wants to date Sherlock Holmes (except maybe John Watson).
- Don't give mixed signals. Make sure your yes means yes and your no means no! People who are hot and cold are just plain confusing.
- Don't give that special someone the silent treatment. Maybe your mom told you, "If you can't say anything nice, don't say anything at all." But sometimes

you've got to speak up, even when what
you have to say is hard to hear.

• Don't give ultimatums. They're mean,
and they don't work anyway.

We'll spend the rest of this chapter
unpacking why people make these common
mistakes and what you could do instead.

"What's an ultimatum?" Arav asked the room.

Jamal shrugged. Ramirez muttered "dunno." But
Andrew said, "It's when you make someone do what you
want by threatening them."

He remembered Eve saying, *You have to sit with us, or I'll
tell everyone . . .*

"Dude, that's messed up." Ramirez punctuated the state-
ment with a three-count roll.

Andrew thought about Eve acting fake-sad all the
way to school, not wanting to talk about it, accusing him
of thinking about other girls, giving him a dozen yeses last
night and then a great big silent NO today. He slammed the
book down. "Eve's been doing *all* this stuff."

"What the—"

"That is sick."

"Why would she do that?" Arav asked.

"Because she's an actual trash bag?" Jamal offered.

"Dump her. Text her now and do it," Ramirez commanded.

"That's too good for her," Jamal countered. "Like, she belongs in juvy."

Andrew couldn't text right now. He couldn't even speak. This felt like a Judas kiss. Utter betrayal.

This whole time, Eve had been playing mind games. She was literally taking instructions for how to be horrible from a book and then using them to torture him. Friends don't do that. *People* don't do that. She wasn't even Eve anymore. She was this evil mutant version of herself that enjoyed making his life a living hell.

He felt like he'd just found out he was a lab rat. A psychology experiment. He felt like he was in the Hunger Games arena and Eve was shooting fireballs at him from the production room.

Andrew had never been really and truly mad at Eve before, in all the years they'd been friends. His mom said he had a "long fuse." At first Andrew thought that meant nothing ever bothered him, which wasn't true. But then he found out that a fuse was the string you light on fireworks, and the more explosives are in it, the longer that string needs to be so you don't blow yourself up. That made more sense. He could put up with a lot. But when he'd had enough, he could explode.

He could feel it sizzling now, that fuse in his brain. He'd had just about enough of Eve's head games. She ignored him and then smothered him. She texted him kissy faces and then yelled at him for even looking at her. She purposely humiliated him in front of his friends. Stole his favorite hoodie. Got half the school calling him Andy Wandy. Blackmailed him. Threatened to make him wear a diaper in public. Acted like she wanted to kiss him and then ghosted him the next day.

"AAAAAAARGH!!" Andrew threw his mallet like a javelin. It hit the door with a loud *crack*.

The guys' conversation and the ever-present noise of the drumline went instantly silent. Jamal, Ramirez, and Arav all looked at him with wide eyes and open mouths. But nobody said anything.

Throwing the stick hadn't even taken the edge off Andrew's fury. He hoisted his backpack with a growl, stalked toward the door, and kicked it open.

"Bruh, where you going?" Ramirez asked, sounding worried.

"To get some forks." Andrew snatched up his broken mallet and let the door slam behind him.

Chapter 23
Walk Away

Eve had just enough energy to hold her head high and strut until she was out of sight of the school. But as soon as she was sure no one could judge her, she dropped the diva walk. And she ran.

It was a cold, windy day. Tears froze on her cheeks.

She thought about her mom saying, *Sometimes you've got to know when to walk away.* Had Andrew's mom given him the same advice? Had he realized she just wasn't worth the effort?

She *had* been horrible. But only because she was trying to save her family. Why did he give up on her just when she was starting to realize her mistakes? She'd thought their friendship could survive anything.

But he'd been gross and confusing and frustrating. This wasn't all her fault. He'd changed so much this summer. Maybe one of the changes was that he'd turned from a great person into a total player.

She tried to make herself believe that.

Mostly, she wanted her mom.

Eve didn't slow her pace until she hit her driveway. As soon as she got inside the house, she called, "Mom?"

No answer.

A little louder, she called, "Mom?!"

She thought she heard a muffled "Up here," so she pounded up the stairs. She found her mom in her parents' bedroom.

Packing.

"Mom?"

Her mom was emptying her medicine cabinet into an overnight bag. She grunted in greeting but didn't look away from her task. Day cream. Night cream. Serum. Toothpaste. It all went into the bag.

An alarm blared in Eve's head. *Warning. Warning. Maximum payload exceeded.*

"What's going on?" Eve managed to whisper.

"I'm going to stay with Auntie Jen." She threw her makeup bag into the suitcase. "Just to clear my head."

Eve couldn't breathe. She wheezed, "That's in *Nebraska*."

"I'll be back in a couple weeks."

Eve didn't believe her.

"Just a couple weeks," her mom repeated. It didn't even sound like she believed herself. "Hey—be sure to send me pictures of you and Andrew on Halloween, okay?" She closed the distance between them and hugged Eve tight.

"Don't go," Eve pleaded.

"I love you," Mom said, and Eve knew that meant goodbye.

Eve sat in her room composing texts to Andrew.

my mom left

idk what to do

please come

I know I've been a crappy friend lately but I really need to talk to you

SOS

hey Andrew r u still up?

She didn't send any of them. When it came down to it, she didn't know how to let him see her bleeding heart when she was pretty sure he'd already replaced her. Maybe he was with Madison right now, flirting or making out or doing algebra. Maybe he was leaning toward her under a streetlight.

She told herself that she didn't need to tell him anyway. He'd hear about it through the mom-grapevine. Or he'd notice that her mom's car was gone. Or he'd just look at her face tomorrow and know how she was feeling. Like he always had.

If the Andrew who used to be her friend was still in there somewhere, he'd show up when she needed him.

And that was now.

Eve fought with her dad the next morning.

"I'm NOT going!"

"Eve, stop it!" Dad slammed her insulated lunch bag onto the counter. "I'm going to work, and you're not staying home alone."

"I'm *thirteen*!" Eve shouted. "I'm old enough to stay home by myself! I *can't* go to school today!"

"Get in the car. I'll drive you." Dad looked grim. Like he was placing her under arrest.

"So now you don't even trust me to walk on my own?"

Eve was furious. Her mom had left them just over twelve hours ago, and her dad had already become the classic overbearing dictator father.

"Eve, this conversation is OVER. Get. In. The. Car."

With a growl, Eve snatched up the lunch bag that her mom should have packed. She stomped through the garage where her mom's car should have been and sat in the passenger seat of the Charger that her mom called her dad's "midlife crisis mobile."

School was a cold, silent, five-minute drive away. When her dad pulled up to the curb, she got out and slammed the door without saying goodbye. Then she walked into the school with only one goal for the day: *do not cry.*

She would be angry. She might even be mean. But she would *not* have a breakdown in public. Crying was for when she was alone in her room. She'd done plenty of it last night. But at school she wasn't even going to show a hint of sadness that might make someone say the words "What's wrong?" Sympathy might crack her armor. And she would never *ever* be the crying-in-the-bathroom girl. She might be the Dad's-going-to-be-sorry-he-sent-me-to-school-because-I-punched-someone-and-got-suspended girl, though.

Someone like Mateo Ramirez. He came swaggering toward her looking especially punchable with an evil grin on his face. She didn't wait for him to do something disgusting.

She snarled from ten feet away, "Not *one* word. I will end you."

He veered away looking nervous.

Later, she gave Jamal and Arav such a scathing look that they stopped their conversation and backed into the wall of lockers to let her pass.

At lunch Sofia made the mistake of asking, "Are you and Andrew going to sit together today?"

"How about if you don't ask me about him every freaking day?" Eve snapped.

Sofia looked like she might cry, and Eve felt like a puppy kicker.

Thankfully, Destiny retorted, "Girl needs to find her happy place."

That helped Eve hang on to anger so she didn't have to face any not-safe-for-school feelings like regret, shame, or sorrow. She growled, "No one asked."

A couple of minutes later Andrew walked past their table and glared at her like she'd broken his drum kit. How dare he? *He* was the one who was flirting with someone else. She glared back so hard, she was surprised he didn't burst into flames.

So much for her friend showing up when she needed him. Now that she knew she loved him—the old him—it was too late.

The thing was, now that the worst had happened with her mom, she should just break up with Andrew. She'd thought that dating him would make her mom happy and somehow fix her parents' relationship. It didn't.

But then Eve thought about that comment her mom had made practically on her way out the door. . . . *Send me pictures of you and Andrew on Halloween.* Could she somehow get her mom back by hanging on with Andrew just a little bit longer?

Chapter 24

Not Eggs-actly What the Boy Had in Mind

Eve glaring and snarling at him and being rude to his friends for no reason relit the charred remnants of Andrew's burned-down fuse. It made every bite of his lunch bitter. Every joke a little cutting. The drumbeats of the rest of his day were jangled and jarring.

Andrew found that his anger had morphed from Tuesday's bottle rocket into one of those fountain fireworks that showered sparks for a long, *long* time. Mallet-throwing rage had cooled to the kind of seething need for justice that Andrew knew fueled the backstory of just about every great superhero.

When he said good night to his parents Friday night, pretending everything was normal, he felt like Peter Parker. He lay in his bed, eyes wide open in the dark like Daredevil.

Instead of the old gray T-shirt he usually slept in, he wore all black, like Batman.

Next to the bed, his backpack concealed a random assortment of plastic forks that his mom had saved from every birthday party and take-out place, his broken mallet, and a photo of him and Eve laughing at the park in their fancy purple outfits. A few days ago he thought he'd cherish the picture forever. Now it was just a reminder of how she had sabotaged their entire relationship.

Andrew listened to the clock ticking and waited for the signal.

When he saw the light of Ramirez's flashlight flicking on and off close to midnight, he had zero qualms about sliding on the backpack and slipping out the back door to join him. Keeping to the shadows, he made his way to the side of his house. He had to crouch low to stay under the windows as he jogged toward where the light had come from. Yeah, his parents were in bed and the house was dark, but why take chances?

Ramirez and Holden were waiting for him under the oak tree in the front yard. The same tree that had dropped millions of leaves for him and Eve to rake up and jump into, once upon a time.

All three guys were wearing black, just like they'd planned. Well, Andrew's jacket was dark blue. It was the best he could do on short notice. Between the secret signal, the stealth meeting, and the wardrobe, they were basically Avengers. Andrew's heart pounded, and he felt more awake than he had since the Harvest Festival.

"Ready?" Ramirez whispered.

Holden nodded once, displaying a box of five hundred forks he'd brought. Andrew dipped his chin too, for once not minding Holden's contribution. Ramirez gave a military-looking wave that universally meant *move out*. And the three boys made their way across the street, avoiding the glow from the streetlight and glancing around for threats.

Eve's porch light came on the moment they reached the driveway. The boys froze, momentarily blinded and sure they'd been caught. For a second Andrew panicked, but then he remembered that the light had a motion sensor. It didn't mean anyone had noticed they were here. He cuffed Ramirez's arm and mouthed, *Motion sensor*.

Ramirez and Holden visibly relaxed. Holden opened the fork box, and they all filled their pockets and fists. Then, aided by the porch light, they spread across the yard with their tools of justice. Jamming the forks into the ground was satisfying. Sometimes a tine or two snapped off, but mostly they stuck easily. When the boys ran out of forks, they fell back to the sidewalk to survey their work. Five hundred and twenty-two white plastic monuments to freedom.

Just to make sure Eve got the message, Andrew pulled two more things out of his jacket pocket—the broken mallet and the photo. He speared the jagged stick through the photo and dug it into the ground at his feet. The guys retreated back across the street to the oak tree and fist-bumped their victory, before Ramirez and Holden got onto their bikes and rode off in opposite directions.

It took a long time for Andrew's heart to stop beating fast. Even longer for him to fall asleep. Then, after what felt like only a few seconds, he was jolted awake by a *crunch* and *splat*. The morning sun streamed through the slats in his blinds. He blinked and rolled over.

Splunch.

There it was again. A wet-sounding crunch. Curiosity overpowering his drowsiness, Andrew sat up, scrubbing his eyes.

Splunch.

He went to the window and pulled the cord to open the blinds. Goo dripped down the glass. Through the film he could see Eve winding up to throw, a half-empty carton of eggs and the crumpled, torn photo in her other hand.

Splunch. Andrew flinched as the egg splattered against the glass inches from his face. He heard shuffling behind him and glanced back to see Tom yawning in the doorframe.

He slid open the window, the frosty morning air waking

him up fast, and called, "I guess you got my message."

"You're a jerk, Andrew!" Eve yelled, her voice thick and gravelly. If he didn't know better, Andrew would have thought she was crying. But Eve never cried. She yelled again, "You're *such* a jerk!"

"HA!" Andrew laughed bitterly. "Look who's talking. You've been a world-class brat to me all year!"

"Then BREAK UP WITH ME!" Eve demanded.

"No," he said reflexively.

"Why not?!"

"Because you're not the boss of me. If you want to break up, you say it." Andrew had no idea why Eve wanted him to break up with her, but he was in no mood to do anything she told him to. Another idea occurred to him, and he added, "You're not gonna make me the bad guy."

"Too late. You already did that to yourself!"

From the corner of his eye, Andrew could see Tom making a cutting motion across his neck and then waving his hands like, *Stop! Danger! Retreat!*

But there was no retreat now. "Suck eggs!" Andrew yelled, slamming the window just in time to keep yolk out of his hair when Eve launched the next egg with equal parts accuracy and rage. The girl had an *arm*.

And a *mouth*. Even through the glass, he could hear her roar, "Fork yourself!"

He was pretty sure she'd said "fork."

He didn't have much time to overthink it, because the next moment he heard, "ANDREW ANNAS OZDEMIR!"

Andrew spent the rest of the day doing hard time. His mom made him pull all the forks out of Eve's yard and comb through the grass on his hands and knees to find "every last tiny shard of plastic, or so help me, Halloween is canceled." Then he had to scrub the egg off his window and the side of the house, which was not fair because that should have been Eve's job. Apparently, she wasn't going to get any punishment at all. And forks were easy to clean up compared to the impenetrable concrete of cold, dried raw-egg slime. He had to use a ladder and scrub brush and about a thousand gallons of water from the hose.

He was wet and exhausted and freezing and *seething* by the time he was done.

But as soon as he changed out of his wet clothes, his dad said he had to work off the cost of a new set of mallets to replace the one he broke. He made Andrew help clean the garage and, to make it worse, spent the whole time lecturing him on "this isn't how we raised you" and "what were you thinking" and "no son of mine . . ."

By the time he collapsed into his bed that night, Andrew was a shell of a man. Everything hurt and he hated the world.

So maybe the forking wasn't the best idea ever. But Eve had driven him to it. All of this was her fault.

"Hey, dude," Tom said, walking in without asking permission and planting himself on the side of the bed.

"What do you want?" Andrew groaned.

"I just want to say that you really got the shaft today."

Through the fog of misery, Andrew felt a swell of appreciation for his brother. Tom was the one person in this family who understood what he was going through. Andrew punched his pillow. "Yeah. Eve is the worst. I can't believe she didn't even get in trouble."

Tom cracked his knuckles. "I've got your back." He clapped Andrew hard on the shoulder, stood, and stretched his arms over his head. "We're gonna make her wish she'd never gone to war with you."

"Change of plans," Reese announced to the friend group two weeks later, while they were all hanging out in the cafeteria before school on Monday. Nina, Destiny, Sofia, and Eve all looked up from their phones. Once she had their attention, Reese said, "Let's all go trick-or-treating with Jamal and his crew."

"Wait! What?!" Eve practically yelled before she pulled herself together and tried to look like not a drama queen. More calmly, she said, "I thought you guys broke up."

"Again," Destiny muttered.

Reese shrugged. "We're back together."

"Aaaw," Sofia cooed. "Yaaaay."

The thing was, Eve had been waiting two weeks to get

her revenge for the forking. Two weeks of avoiding each other and glaring across the lunchroom and sending bogus texts to her mom about how sweet he was being. Two weeks of constantly wondering if he was with Madison.

She didn't see them together. Even the rumor mill had died down. Aside from band, they didn't seem to hang out. Eve was starting to think that maybe he and Madison had never been a thing. But then why was he suddenly so hateful to her? Why did he destroy the photo?

No matter how she looked at it, it didn't quite make sense. He had simultaneously completely rejected and betrayed her and refused to break up with her. It was sick.

So she'd been counting on the girls doing something that she could drag Andrew to as a form of punishment. In the calmest, coolest voice she could muster, Eve said, "What about the haunted house? I thought we were for sure doing that?"

A haunted house would be perfect, because Andrew hated scary stuff.

Reese shrugged. "Jamal invited me to trick-or-treat with them, and I think we should all go."

Sofia interjected, "I really didn't want to do the haunted house anyway. This is great. Do you think Mark will be there?"

Nina said, "Girl, NO! Get a grip!"

Sofia deflated. But Destiny said, "I love trick-or-treating. Where are we going?"

While Reese gave her directions to the neighborhood with the "good candy," Eve shot Nina a look that said, *Help me!* But Nina was clearly swayed by Reese's descriptions of full-sized Snickers and over-the-top yard décor. She said, "Chill out, Eve. It's gonna be great. You got that baby costume ready for you-know-who?"

Eve was torn. She *did* want to punish Andrew for the forking—especially because it came at the worst possible time. Her mom had literally abandoned her, and then, after crying herself to sleep three nights in a row, she'd woken up to Andrew's hateful vandalism. Instead of being there for her when she most needed him, he'd kicked her while she was down. Seriously, who does that?

True, she had egged his house. He totally deserved that. But it wasn't nearly enough punishment to make them equal. So, from one perspective, justice demanded that she make a giant diaper out of a bath towel and force him to wear it around in public. But on the other hand, she had no faith that she could actually force him to do it. And, if she were being *really* honest with herself—which she most definitely did not want to be—she was tired of the war. It felt like every time she punked Andrew, she lost a little piece of her soul. She barely recognized this mean girl she had turned into. If she did the diaper thing, she might end up hating herself even more than Andrew would hate her.

The dilemma was, how could she get back at Andrew without basically creating a Horcrux? The question hung over Eve's head all day. So she was weirdly relieved when she got a text from Andrew after school.

Lil Drummer Boi

> I got our costumes for
> Halloween!! 😏

A part of Eve was suspicious. Why was Andrew suddenly texting like everything was cool between them? But a bigger part of her wanted to pretend with him. She wanted to pretend it together so hard that they could make it be true. So she texted back.

Eve

> what is it?

Lil Drummer Boi

> it's a surprise

> you'll find out tomorrow
> night

Even though she was sure Andrew knew this, she texted:

Eve

I hate surprises

He left that one on "read."

Eve spent twenty-four hours writhing in pre-surprise agony. She tried to tell herself that it might not be so bad. Andrew wasn't *that* mean-spirited. He wasn't creative enough to do anything truly horrible. At least she'd get a good picture to send to her mom.

She was wrong on all counts.

At five o'clock on Halloween, Andrew showed up at her front door with a suspiciously big smile and a plastic bag. He held it out. "Okay, here's your half of the costume. Tom and I found it at Goodwill. It's awesome."

Swallowing back dread, Eve took the fabric out of the bag. She held it out and let it unfurl. It was a full-length, flesh-colored bodysuit with attached fake leaves forming a bikini. Even though she knew, Eve choked out, "What. Is. This."

"I know how much you *love* Adam and Eve jokes—"

She despised them more than anything else. Every single time she had met a new person her *entire life*, the first

187

thing they would say was, "You mean like Adam and Eve?"
And just because her name was Eve, most people thought it
was hilarious to tell her Adam and Eve jokes. Like she hadn't
heard every single one of them a thousand million times. Just
thinking about it made her want to punch a hole in the wall.

Andrew gestured to the costume. "Better get it on.
Jamal's mom is picking us up any minute."

"No."

"Yeah, for real." Andrew seemed to be purposely missing
her outrage. "We agreed to do a couples costume, so . . ."

Eve wadded up the costume and threw it at him. "I'm
not wearing that."

Andrew caught it and let it dangle between them. "You
have to, though, because you're my girlfriend. Unless you
want to break up?"

Finally! It was happening! She'd won! She was still mad
and heartbroken, but also triumphant when she said, "You're
dumping me?"

"Nope," Andrew said firmly. "Are *you* dumping *me*?"

She narrowed her eyes. She was no quitter. There was no
way she would admit defeat after all this time and effort. No
way was she going to be the one to say the words. There was
only one way for this thing to end—Andrew *had* to dump her.

"Absolutely not," she said flatly. She glared at him, waiting. He glared back.

While they were locked in this high-stakes staring competition, Eve's dad walked in. "Hi?" he said.

Eve didn't respond. Didn't even blink.

But Andrew put the Eve costume behind his back—which did nothing to hide it—cleared his throat, and said, "Hi, Mr. McNeil."

Eve congratulated herself on winning the glare-off.

"Whatcha got there?" Dad said.

Andrew's face went puce. "It's just a Halloween costume."

Eve's dad's eyes narrowed in the way they always did right before he gave a direct order or said "absolutely not" to something. The thing was, Eve was still mad at him for making her go to school when she'd needed a mental health day. And for letting mom leave . . . or at least not doing anything to make her stay.

Just thinking about the empty space where her mom should be made Eve feel hollowed out. And her dad acting fine about it made her want to inflict some pain on him. He shouldn't get to be fine.

Dad eyes were still narrowed as he looked at the costume. "That doesn't seem appropriate."

Eve ripped the costume out of Andrew's hand. "Dad, it's just a costume! Chill."

She stomped up the stairs, costume in hand. But once

the door was closed, shutting out the two most frustrating males in her life, Eve found herself alone with the costume. She threw it onto the bed before stepping back to look at it again. It was truly terrible. The color and texture of a dirty Band-Aid. The fake leaves were not only tacky but crumpled and creased. There was a dull brown stain on one knee.

She couldn't make herself put it on.

She jogged from wall to wall a couple of times. What was she going to do? If she didn't wear it, she was basically admitting her dad was right. But if she did wear it, she was letting Andrew win. Either way, how was she going to send a picture to her mom? Suddenly it occurred to Eve that Andrew's costume must be equally embarrassing. If he was going to dress her up in fig leaves, he had to be Adam and wear the same thing. Maybe it would be worth it to call his bluff, just to force him to humiliate himself.

"Fine," Eve said to the empty room. "Whatever."

She changed into a pair of black leggings and a long-sleeve black shirt before putting on the flimsy polyester costume. It was lumpy and saggy, and actually being naked would probably be less embarrassing. Eve almost chickened out and took it back off. But the doorbell announced that Jamal had arrived to pick them up. Eve put her running shoes on and went back downstairs.

The look on her dad's face *almost* made the costume

worth it. His mouth opened and closed like he knew he was supposed to say something, but he didn't know what. He probably wished someone—like her *mom*—would take over and talk sense into his rebellious teenage daughter.

Unfortunately, Andrew's and Jamal's stifled sniggering ruined the moment. She whirled on them, but she wouldn't let them see that they'd gotten to her. She smiled too sweetly.

The boys both clamped their mouths closed. Jamal had regular clothes on but was holding a red Solo cup.

"What are you supposed to be?" Eve asked, shifting the attention away from her abomination of a costume, if only momentarily.

"I'm a frat boy!" Jamal said proudly. He pointed toward the street with his cup. "My mom's waiting."

"Sounds good," Eve said in her perkiest voice. And without giving her father a chance to protest, she said, "Bye, Dad."

"Not too late. It's a school night," he managed to call before she shut the door between them.

The night was getting really cold, and Eve instantly wished she'd brought a coat. It would have kept her warm and covered her horrifying bodysuit. But there was no way she was going back in to get it. That would ruin her decently dignified exit and force her to keep talking to her dad.

Andrew sauntered next to her, bundled in his own winter coat.

Eve stopped him with an arm bar and a singsong, "Okay, show off your costume, and let's take a selfie!"

Andrew blinked at her innocently before unzipping his coat and taking his other hand out of his pocket.

He was holding an apple and wearing a black T-shirt that said, "Bite me."

Chapter 26
Mistakes Were Made

Tom was right about the Original Sin costume. It was a KO. Jamal looked like he might pop a vein trying not to laugh, and for a second Eve looked like she was going to burst out crying. But then she pasted on a happy face and said in her too-high voice, "Good one."

She slung one arm around Andrew's shoulder, held her phone out, and snapped a picture. Then she looked at it and said, "You weren't smiling. Try again." She took another selfie. This time Andrew managed to grimace in a way that might pass for a smile. Eve looked at the picture, and nodded. "For my mom," she explained brightly as she sent it.

Suddenly it occurred to Andrew how weird it was that

Eve's mom hadn't been the one to see them off tonight. When was the last time he had seen her, actually?

"Come on! Let's go!" Jamal called from the curb. As they walked toward him, Jamal bit down on his fist and held his breath, trying not to laugh.

When they reached Jamal's van, Andrew opened the door for Eve, adding a gentlemanly bow. She flashed him her fake smile, but he glimpsed her red-faced scowl as she climbed past him. He could practically hear her think-screaming, *I don't need your boy muscles to open doors for me.* It was a small victory.

So why did he feel like a loser?

Ramirez and Arav were in the middle seats. Ramirez's whole body, wrapped in a long black robe, was shaking with silent hysterical laughter. From under the hood of his fuzzy dinosaur costume, Arav's eyes were huge and his mouth was hanging open. Andrew gave them a nod as he slid in next to Eve.

Jamal sat up front, in the passenger seat, where he continued to wheeze and make squeaking noises.

"Everybody buckled?" his mom called. After a few clicks and yeses, the van started moving.

Eve sat rigidly with her arms crossed over her fake leaves. Andrew sat as far from her as possible, pressing himself against the plastic side panel. He kept feeling like he should say sorry and promise to give her all the candy he got tonight.

But then he'd remember how she'd tormented him with the stuff from that book, and he'd think about scrubbing egg off his house for a thousand hours, and Tom inside his head would bark like a sensei, *Strike fast! Strike hard! No mercy!*

"Hey, Eve." Ramirez turned to look at them over the back of the seat. He was grinning like nobody's business. "You should have read the Apple terms and conditions."

He snorted, and all the guys laughed.

"Real original," Eve snapped.

Ramirez went serious. "You aren't allowed to be in a bad mood on Halloween."

Eve cleared her throat and plastered her smile back on. "Why would I be in a bad mood? I'm awesome!"

Ramirez shrugged, turned around, and said to Arav, "Remember that headless horseman house last year?"

"Yeah. With the red eyes. And the Laffy Taffy," Arav affirmed.

"Andrew wouldn't even go up to the door."

"I don't like Laffy Taffy!" Andrew said in self-defense.

"Yeah, right. You were scared. You're just a wimp."

Andrew couldn't think of a comeback. Once upon a time, Eve would have stuck up for him. Now her lip twitched, turning her plastic smile into a bitter smirk.

"Here we are!" Jamal's mom sang cheerfully.

The moment the van stopped, Ramirez flung himself out

the door and started jumping around like a hype man, calling, "Come on! Let's go! Hurry up!"

Andrew unbuckled and slid out. But when he turned back around, Eve was twisted into a pretzel, unzipping her costume. While he stood gaping, she peeled herself like a banana and left the costume on the floor. When she emerged from the van, she was wearing a black shirt and leggings.

"Okay, guys," Jamal's mom said, leaning out the van window. "Have fun and stay together. Don't leave this neighborhood. Meet me back here in two hours."

They all said they would. Andrew added, "Thanks for driving us, Mrs. Jones."

She smiled at him. "You win all the kindness awards, don't you? You're welcome."

Andrew didn't feel like he deserved any kindness awards. For a second, the urge to tell Eve he was sorry was overwhelming.

But she was already running down the street. Andrew realized Reese, Sofia, Destiny, and Nina were standing in a clump at the corner.

Arav, Jamal, and Ramirez gathered around Andrew.

"She's being weird," Ramirez said.

"Yeah," Andrew mumbled. "The costume was maybe a bad idea."

"I thought it was hilarious," Jamal said.

"She seemed okay on the way here," Arav added.

"I'm pretty sure that was her game face," Andrew said, scrubbing at his hair. "She hates the costume. She's still mad about the forking, too."

"Just don't ruin Halloween," Ramirez said, his voice muffled as he slid his plague doctor mask over his face. "I'll be seriously ticked."

Jamal started walking toward the girls, gesturing with his red cup for the guys to follow. "Let's do this!"

Reese, wearing a tutu and zombie makeup, slid her hand into Jamal's and smiled at him as he reached her side. Andrew felt a stab of . . . something. He remembered Eve looking at him like that and the way they'd moved together for one moment under the streetlight. How she'd felt in his arms and how the wind played with her hair. Something lurched in his stomach. He reminded himself that she'd just been playing some sick game with him—nothing from that night was real.

"What are you guys supposed to be?" Destiny asked, looking from Eve to Andrew from under an enormous witch's hat.

Andrew had planned to say, *A big mistake*, whenever someone asked that tonight. But since Eve had taken off her costume, the joke didn't really make sense anymore. He looked at his apple. "Uh."

"He's Edward and I'm Bella," Eve said.

The girls instantly started talking over each other.

"I get it! Bite me! Because he's a vampire!"

"The apple! From the cover! Perfect!"

"Aaaaw, so romantic."

Andrew looked down at his "Bite Me" shirt, grudgingly impressed. How did Eve think of this stuff so fast? On the other hand, the last thing Andrew wanted to be for Halloween—or ever really—was the creepy stalker vampire guy from *Twilight*. He'd never seen the movie, but he'd watched a reaction video on YouTube once, and that was bad enough.

Then Holden swaggered up with a butcher knife apparently speared through his head. Gross. Andrew felt instantly annoyed.

Andrew gritted his teeth and tried to do the thing Eve was so good at—act totally fine when she really wanted to punch somebody. It was way harder than Eve made it look.

There was a round of heys, and Ramirez gave Holden a fist bump. Holden held his fist toward Andrew—acting like they were buds now that they had vandalized something together. Reluctantly, Andrew bumped his fist against Holden's. It felt like betraying himself. He wished Eve hadn't been there to see it.

Then Holden wedged his way into the girls' semicircle, bobbed his eyebrows at Destiny, and said, "You're a hot witch."

She gave him the stink eye. Andrew really thought she

might punch him. He wouldn't mind seeing that.

"You guys, let's go!" Ramirez was antsy for candy.

"Uh." Andrew scratched his head. "I think Madison is coming. We should wait for her."

Every pair of eyes was on him with varying degrees of questions, accusations, and even—from Sofia—genuine worry. There was a V between Eve's eyebrows that made him want to apologize all over again, even though he had just been trying to include Madison to be friendly. And then Holden said, "Daaaawg."

Why did this have to be a big deal?

Arav rescued him. "Oh yeah, we invited her, remember? She told me she was for sure coming."

Now everyone turned their eyeball questions on Arav. He answered them all with a shrug.

Ramirez barely had time to finish a long groan before a car pulled up and Madison got out. She was wearing a shimmery green bodysuit and lots of green eyeshadow. She even had green lipstick on.

After a few heys and hellos, Arav said, "What are you supposed to be?"

"I'm a snake," Madison said proudly.

Eve choked. "*What?!*"

Jamal made a long low *hoooooooooo* sound. Arav had a coughing fit.

Ramirez threw up his hands with an exasperated, "Halloween is ruined." He stalked off alone, clutching his pillowcase against his black robes.

It took Andrew a second to catch on.

And then it hit him.

Everyone thought he had gotten Madison to be a snake as part of the Original Sin costume. Like she was Eve's nemesis or something. His eyes met Eve's for a second that stretched on and on—long enough for him to see heartbreak turn into hatred before her game face snapped back into place.

He felt his whole body go hot like a cartoon thermometer. His face was going to set itself on fire for sure. He wanted to shout that it was a total coincidence, that he wouldn't do that to Eve even if she tortured him for a lifetime. But it came out, "Uh."

"I don't get it," Nina announced unapologetically.

"Me neither," Madison said.

Destiny shook her head, and Sofia shrugged. None of them had seen the Original Sin costume.

"It's nothing," Eve snapped. "They're just being toddlers." Then she marched away in the opposite direction from Ramirez.

Everyone else was left to pick sides. Destiny and Nina exchanged eye rolls before Nina commanded, "Come on." They went after Eve, taking Sofia with them.

Reese watched them go with a pained look on her face, still holding Jamal's hand. He leaned in. "You wanna just do our own thing?" Reese nodded, and they meandered away, leaving Arav, Madison, Holden, and Andrew to awkwardly avoid looking at each other.

"Wow, guys. Thanks for inviting me," Madison said with heavy sarcasm. "It's been awesome so far."

Andrew scratched his head, which was suddenly itching like crazy. He wasn't even sure how Halloween had crashed and burned so fast, but it seemed like it was his fault.

Arav cleared his throat. "Let's catch up with Ramirez."

They spent the rest of the time going door-to-door, actively avoiding Eve's group, and trying hard to fill awkward silences by talking about drumline. Glow Night was in a few days, and they all agreed it was going to be the most epic thing ever.

Trying to get excited about anything was like lifting weights with Tom in the garage—it took a ton of effort and concentration, and Andrew mostly couldn't wait for it to be over. But he wouldn't let the crew down. Glow Night was probably the most important thing to all of them. Maybe to the whole school. He *had* to be all in.

The thing between him and Eve had somehow escaped containment and made a mess of Halloween—not just for them, but for their friends, too. But Glow Night would be different. Glow Night would be amazing.

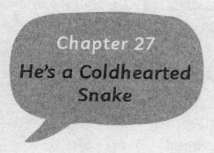

Chapter 27
He's a Coldhearted Snake

It took all of Eve's concentration to go through the motions of trick-or-treating. With no coat, she was shivering. Inside, she was miserable. And the girls trying to empathize were making it so much harder to act cool about everything.

First, they badgered her with "Are you okay?" and "What's going on?" until she gave in and told them about the Eve-and-the-apple costume. Destiny went, "Nuh-*uh*," produced a black eyeliner, and painted a cat nose and whiskers on Eve's face. Then they spent the microwalks between houses analyzing what Andrew had done, instead of letting her pretend she was fine.

"So not only does he like someone else—he's basically throwing it in her face!" Destiny pointed out to the group.

I'm still here, thought Eve.

"Seriously," Nina agreed. "Turning a couples costume into a three-way costume? Who does that?"

Sofia ventured, "There *must* be a mistake. Maybe—"

"No," Nina insisted. "He's a monster. And now he's trick-or-treating with *her* instead of his girlfriend? Literal pond scum."

"I tried to warn you," Destiny said. "You should never talk to him again."

Eve didn't respond. She was afraid if she tried, she'd burst out crying. So she stuffed a wad of gummy worms into her mouth as a good excuse to just nod along.

She tried not to think about Andrew and Madison trick-or-treating together. Was he holding her hand right now? *Don't think about it.*

It was better to stay mad. So while she went door-to-door, Eve focused on everything Andrew had done to her and all the kinks in his soul. The fig leaves, the forks, the photo, the fart tag . . . and now pitting her against Madison.

The Andrew she used to be best friends with never would have done any of that stuff. But that Andrew was gone. He'd been replaced by Dark Matter Andrew. Dark Matter Andrew was cocky, manipulative, cruel, and incapable of human feelings. She recited all of it inside her head, converting grief and humiliation into anger—like the fusion constantly burning in a star's core.

By the time they had returned to their designated meeting spot, Eve felt like she was on the brink of a supernova. Jamal's mom was already parked and waiting for them with the sliding van door open. Eve climbed to her spot in the back and slumped in the corner, trying to warm up. Trying to decide how to act toward Andrew when he sat next to her.

Shunning him was the obvious choice. But maybe that just proved he'd gotten to her. Maybe she should smile and act happy so he'd think she didn't even care what he did or who he hung out with.

Before Eve had fully committed to either plan, her phone dinged with an incoming text alert.

Mom

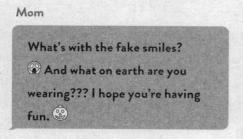

What's with the fake smiles? 😱 And what on earth are you wearing??? I hope you're having fun. 🎃

Should she tell her mom that Andrew had humiliated her and broken her heart? Maybe Mom would feel sorry for her and come home. Or maybe her mom had a maximum payload like Eve did, and she wouldn't be able to handle Eve's drama on top of everything else she was dealing with.

Maybe she would only want to come home if Eve was happy and fun.

Maybe there was no right answer. Nothing she could do.

She was still staring at the text when Andrew strolled up, flanked by Madison, Mateo, Holden, and Arav. Instead of getting in right away, they stood in a clump right outside the van, talking excitedly.

" . . . play a *giant* game of keep-it-up with white balloons," Holden was saying.

Eve shivered in the dark.

Arav said, "Mr. Handen said they got like a thousand glow-in-the-dark paintballs. It's going to be five dollars for ten paintballs, and you throw them at the wall. Like a mural."

"Like a Jackson Pollock painting," Madison corrected.

Holden and Mateo both went, "Cool!"

Madison was more pragmatic. "As long as it's after our part. If *one* person gets paint on our drum kits . . . I'm not kidding."

Andrew said, "Yeah. That would be bad."

The anger-fusion inside Eve intensified. Andrew refused to break up with her, but was perfectly fine with standing five feet from her talking to the girl he *obviously* preferred over her. Acting like he had no memory of them ever being friends.

Eve couldn't let herself think about how things used to be. It hurt too much to remember everything she had lost.

And now she had nothing to look forward to but rejection, humiliation, loneliness, and custody hearings.

She couldn't even look forward to Glow Night. She didn't want to go anymore. Why would she? It would just be another opportunity for her to see how happy Andrew was with all his other friends and how easily he had replaced her.

When everyone clambered into the van, Eve stared hard out her window. She didn't even look at Andrew the whole way home. They both climbed out when Jamal's mom stopped the van in front of Andrew's house. He hesitated and said, "Um. Eve—"

"Don't," Eve whispered. That one syllable was all she could manage. She ran home before Andrew could see her armor crack.

Chapter 28
Gross Candy and Bad Advice

Andrew slammed through the door and hurled his candy bag to the floor. This was officially the worst night of his life. Tom had made it seem like getting back at Eve would be hilarious. And she definitely deserved it. Andrew had thought it would feel like victory.

But all he'd done was prove that Eve was right about him—he really was a jerk.

And then Madison showed up and made everything a hundred times worse. Not that it was her fault. But he just wished she had worn literally any other costume.

Eve wouldn't even let him apologize. *Don't*, she'd said. And her voice had cracked because that word was packed with more hurt and betrayal than one word could hold.

"Hi, Andrew! Did you have fu—" Andrew's mom's face went from cheerful to concerned as she walked in from the kitchen. He was standing there doing nothing, so he didn't know how his mom knew something was wrong. She asked, "What's the matter?"

Andrew shrugged. "Nothing."

"Not nothing," Mom countered, coming around to rub his back. "Need to talk?"

"It's just friend stuff."

His mom let it drop with an "Okay." She picked up his candy bag and looked inside. "Nice haul this year. Can I help you sort it?"

Andrew shrugged again but sat on the floor when she did and let her dump out the bag between them. There was something comforting about this ritual. Every year they looked at all his Halloween candy together, and his mom took the gross stuff.

"Ooh, a Cow Tale!" Mom set it aside.

Andrew half-heartedly piled up the full-sized candy bars. "Where is everyone?"

"Dad's upstairs on a video chat with Uncle Omer. And Tom won't be back for hours. He and—what's the new girlfriend's name? Ella? Anyway, they went to that big haunted house in Oswego."

"Oh." Andrew shuddered. He'd made the mistake of

going to a haunted house that the Band Boosters put on two years ago. There was fake blood everywhere, body parts, and horrible screaming and howling noises. Eve had to practically carry him out, and then he'd had nightmares for days. Everyone but Eve had made fun of him.

The memory of how Eve used to have his back slammed into him. He missed *them*. He wished he could go back to before eighth grade and erase everything that had happened over the past two months. But much fresher memories piled on top of the old ones.

Her running toward him at the airport. The feel of her in his arms. The way she took his breath away in her purple dress and just by looking at him under the streetlight. The way she could make even math fun. The almost kiss.

But then. Glaring and mood swings, threats and accusations, mind games, and raw eggs . . . It was like Evil Eve had murdered his friend, real Eve, and then forced him to do horrible things in self-defense. And he hated her for all of it.

He. Hated. Eve. The truth burned, but not like a firecracker. Like swallowing battery acid.

"Raisinets!" Mom chirped, picking them from the pile.

Andrew swiped at his nose with his sleeve and sniffed. The battery-acid burning was in his throat and behind his eyes.

"I haven't heard any Eve stories lately," Mom said casually, peeling the wrapper off a piece of black licorice.

Andrew shrugged, concentrating hard on the candy pile. He should eat some of it. But nothing looked good, and his stomach was churning.

Mom waited.

When Andrew couldn't stand it anymore, he admitted, "She hates me, Mom. We're not even friends anymore."

It was part of the truth.

"Why would you say that?"

"She's always mad at me. She's mean to me on purpose. She doesn't talk to me or even *look* at me. She got everyone at school to call me Andy."

Mom cringed. "Did you guys break up?"

"No."

Andrew prayed she wouldn't ask any of her usual clarifying questions. He didn't want to have to explain it.

Mom was quiet, which basically proved God was real. She dragged her fingers through the candy, picked out a butterscotch, and added it to her little pile. She seemed to pick her next words just as carefully. "If she hated you, she'd break up with you. I think this probably isn't really about you."

Andrew could only gape at her. She clearly did not understand anything about girls or relationships or Eve or him or eighth grade or life.

She sighed. "It's not my place to give specifics, but Eve's dealing with some things right now. Maybe ask her how she's doing."

"I can't. I told you—she hates me." Andrew smashed a marshmallow ghost inside its wrapper. "She thinks I'm a jerk."

"Well," Mom said, still chewing her licorice. "You *did* fork her yard."

"Mom."

She sighed. "Sometimes we're the cruelest to the people we love the most. We take things out on them and show them the worst parts of us."

"Are you seriously saying that Eve is horrible to me because she *loves* me?"

Now it was Mom's turn to shrug. "Have you tried *talking* to her?"

"Of *course* I tried talking to her."

Or at least he'd meant to. He'd wanted to talk to her so many times. But he couldn't find the words. Or the right timing. Or the texting got weird. Or there were too many people around. Or things were good for one minute, and he didn't want to mess it up. And then, after a while he didn't even want to talk to someone so mean and evil. Why talk to someone he hated? How could words fix anything now? His mom made talking sound so much simpler than it was in real life.

He summarized all those mixed-up thoughts with, "It's too late anyway."

Mom gave him The Look—the one that meant *I am serious, young man*. "Eve needs you to be a good friend right now. You've got to figure out how to do that."

What the heck? Why was his mom taking Eve's side? Wasn't his own mother supposed to be on Team Andrew? He clamped his teeth together.

"Look," Mom exclaimed, picking up something that looked kind of like a Tootsie Roll. "Bit-O-Honey! I didn't know they still made these."

The thing is, even if his mom wasn't wrong, there was no way to do what she said. He wasn't Eve's friend. Not anymore. There was nothing left to figure out. He had tried so hard to save their friendship and get back to what they'd had before. But Eve had changed too much. She seemed determined not only to kill their friendship, but to shred his self-esteem, too. All he wanted now was to stand up to her—because that's how you deal with bullies.

Seriously, why was he even wasting energy feeling bad about the costumes disaster? She had no right to be mad at him. Even if it had been on purpose, she deserved that and worse for everything she'd done to him.

Andrew scooped up a handful of good candy and trudged up the stairs, announcing, "I'm going to bed."

"But it's only seven thirty."

"Then I'm going to listen to angry music and play *Halo*."

"Okay," Mom said, sounding more amused than she should. "Night, honey."

Chapter 29
Glow like You Wanna Glow

The Saturday after Halloween, Eve found her dad sitting at the kitchen table with a cup of coffee. He didn't say good morning, just nodded to her without smiling and then went back to staring at his phone.

There was no way Eve was going to pathetically sit in silence with her dad all morning. So she took her toast to the rarely used dining room. The problem was that Andrew's house was basically the only thing she could see out the dining room windows. There was a crack in the driveway in the exact spot where she had traced Andrew with sidewalk chalk that time they had tried to convince the babysitter that there had been a murder. The details of the memory came back in pieces. The babysitter made them pancakes for dinner and played board games with them. Andrew's parents and her parents had gone on a double date. They used to do that a lot. Back when her parents wanted to spend time together.

Eve forced herself to look away from the window. She didn't want to remember anymore. She got out her phone and texted the group chat that she wasn't going to Glow Night. She was in no mood to party. And she couldn't face Andrew yet—Halloween was still too fresh.

The rest of the day she scrolled through the TV options without finding a single thing to watch, ate Halloween candy, and didn't bother to change out of her pajamas or brush her teeth.

At 6:20 the doorbell rang. Eve ignored it. It was probably a package or something.

It rang again.

"Eve, get the door," her dad called from the den. "I'm on the phone."

Eve was irritated that she had to get off the couch (seriously, what was wrong with Dad's legs?). And then she was genuinely confused when she found Nina, Destiny, and Sofia on her front porch.

"Get dressed," Nina commanded. "You're coming with us to Glow Night."

"Didn't you get my text? I'm not—"

"Yeah, we got it," Destiny said, her tone clearly saying, *and ignored it.*

Eve stood stunned in the doorway until she could hear her mom's voice in her head yelling, *You're letting all the cold air in!* Even though her mom was gone, Eve still felt compelled to close the door. She sighed and stepped back. "Come in."

She should tell her friends that her mom left her. But she couldn't get the words to form. If she said it out loud, then it would be real, part of her identity. Irrevocable. *This is Eve; she lives with her dad. Eve's a little extra, but, you know, her mom left. Poor Eve.*

Maybe next week she'd tell them. Maybe never.

Without warning, Sofia threw her arms around Eve in a tight hug. "You must be sad. It's really hard. But we want you to come with us." Just as abruptly, she let her go.

Destiny put her hands on her hips. "Yeah, tonight is gonna be fire. Don't let the stuff with Andrew make you miss out on the coolest thing ever. Don't give him your power."

Eve chewed her lip, surveying her ratty T-shirt and pajama bottoms. She wasn't physically or emotionally prepared to go anywhere. But it was really nice of the girls to come here and try to drag her out. And the other option was sitting around this sad house with her sullen father, a gaping hole where her mom was supposed to be, and a perfect view of her ex-best friend's house.

Maybe she could go to Glow Night and forget everything else for a couple of hours. But Andrew was going to be there performing. Was she really just going to pretend that Halloween hadn't happened and everything was cool? Her stomach churned with the hurt of betrayal just thinking about what he'd put her through.

"And look," Nina said, holding up a small gift bag with a happy jack-o'-lantern on it. "We made you something special for the occasion."

"Whaaaa—" Eve took the bag, really curious about what it could be. She reached in and pulled out a black T-shirt. When she unfolded it, she saw that it said, in hand-painted neon-yellow letters: "ANDY O is a total player."

Grinning wickedly, Nina and Destiny unzipped their coats to reveal their own DIY black T-shirts. Nina's said, "Boycott Andy." And Destiny's said, "Andrew Ozdemir SUCKS."

With a nudge from Nina, Sofia unzipped her coat, looking conflicted. Her shirt just had a frowny face.

Nina shrugged apologetically. "That was the meanest thing we could get her to write. Sorry."

Eve found herself smiling, her bitterness softened by this act of loyalty from her friends. It was a great feeling to have friends rally around her. "Well, I guess I *have* to go now," she said. "I can't not wear this shirt."

Destiny whooped. Nina fist pumped, and then commanded, "Hurry up and get ready! It starts at seven."

At 7:10, the girls walked into the school gymnasium shoulder to shoulder, like people in movies who are about to go kick butt. Eve imagined they were moving in slo-mo. "Welcome to the Jungle" blasted over the sound system.

The whole gym was black-lit, making everything dark-colored practically disappear but everything white or neon glow. The backdrops they had painted were hung around the walls, shining with their messages and emojis and Eve's twenty-foot-long solar system. Eve spotted her angry Jupiter right away. It looked even more threatening now that it was glowing in the dark.

Luminescent white balloons were bouncing around over the heads of the crowd, and Sofia batted one that came close to them.

There was a booth with a neon sign advertising THE BIGGEST SPLATTER PAINTING IN THE WORLD! MADE BY YOU! $5 TO THROW 10 GLOW-BALLS.

Another booth advertised glow sticks for one dollar each.

There was a big group of kids jumping around in a strobe-lit mosh pit near the dark, empty stage.

Destiny yelled, "THIS IS AWESOME!" over the noise

of the party. Her teeth and even the whites of her eyes glowed under the black lights.

"THIS IS THE BEST THING THAT HAS EVER HAPPENED TO ME!" Nina shouted back.

Holden broke away from a group of band kids and swaggered toward them. Destiny shook her head, pointed away from them, and yelled, "KEEP WALKING!" She turned to the girls and added, "I swear if that guy comes at me tonight, I cannot be held responsible."

Holden stopped out of arm's reach, but caressed his own chin with his finger and thumb like he was still trying to impress them. There was silent consensus among the girls to pointedly ignore him.

"Welcome to the Jungle" faded out and was replaced by the steady beat of a single drum.

The giant garage-door-looking thing that normally separated the stage from the gymnasium was open, and the drumline marched onto the stage to loud applause. They all stepped in time to the simple drumbeat and took their places—the quads front and center, the snares on either side of them, and bass drums and cymbals behind.

There was an audible collective gasp. Even Eve—who had come determined to ignore Andrew and not let him ruin her night—found herself open-mouthed and wide-eyed. Bright white drums stood out against their black jeans and

T-shirts. They had wrapped their drumsticks in white tape. Their faces were highlighted with neon war paint. And they had gelled their hair with something neon. Madison had a bright orange fauxhawk. Mateo looked like a fluorescent green-haired troll doll. Andrew's nearly black hair stood up in yellow-tipped spikes.

They stood with their feet apart and their chins up, looking aggressively cool. As soon as they were all in formation, Madison called, "Good Times," hit the rim of her drum four times, and they launched into a familiar cadence.

Their sticks became glowing white blurs. The sound of all the drums in perfect unison was almost deafening inside the gym. It vibrated through Eve's whole body. She couldn't take her eyes off Andrew. He was concentrating and confident and obviously having fun. He had *skill*. Next to him, Madison was his perfect match. Eve admitted to herself miserably that they looked exactly right together.

There was something about people who loved what they were doing as much as they did—it was like a magic spell over everyone in the room. People were cheering and jumping around.

But every beat felt like it was chiseling through Eve's armor and making cracks in her heart. Pretty soon the cadence in her head was *don't cry—don't cry—don't—don't—don't—don't cry*. She bit her lip and clenched her fists.

Nina elbowed her, and Eve turned to see her pointing to the zipper on her coat. All the girls nodded their understanding. It was time to send a message. *This is what I need,* thought Eve. *To stand up for myself instead of wallowing.* It was better to be sassy than sad.

The girls all took off their coats as the last beats of the cadence resonated through the gym. Eve glanced to either side and saw all of their shirts blazing under the black light. "Andrew Ozdemir SUCKS." "Boycott Andy." "ANDY O is a total player."

"OH MY GOSH! THERE'S MARK!" Sofia squealed. "I HAVE TO HIDE!" She frantically scooped up all their coats—which was both the perfect mobile hiding spot and a great excuse to head toward the door where there was a big coat pile.

Nina took charge. "Whatever. The rest of y'all—girls stand united!"

They linked arms, squared up with the stage, and waited. Eve's heart pounded hard. She didn't know if it was because of the loud drums, the adrenaline of taking a stand, or the unavoidable feeling that she was doing something mean and terrible. Anyway, there was no time to process all the feelings right now.

Andrew looked around at the cheering crowd, engulfed by their adoration. It was like the drumline guys were actual rock stars. And he was drunk on fame. Eve saw the moment when he noticed her. His gaze paused on her, and his eyes narrowed. With his war paint on, he looked genuinely intimidating. A shiver ran through Eve. She lifted her chin defiantly. He smirked.

Andrew held up his sticks, his arms extended in a giant V. The crowd got the message that he had something to say and started to decrease its volume. People shushed each other. After a few seconds, Andrew said loudly, "Thanks for coming out, everybody. We hope you're enjoying Glow Night."

The kids cheered again.

Eve ground her teeth. How dare he make a speech like it was *his* Glow Night? She and her friends had done just as much as anybody else to make tonight happen.

Andrew waited for the cheering to die down and then said, "We've been working on a new cadence. Do you wanna hear it?"

The school cheered that they did.

Andrew grinned, his teeth glowing, and Eve swore he looked right at her. He shouted, "I want to dedicate this one to Eve McNeil. It's called 'Two-Faced.'"

The whole crowd went, *"Ooooooh."* The universal response to a sick burn.

And then Madison did a four-beat count-off, and they

started to drum. *BUM—tica-tica-tica-tica BUM duh duh BUM . . .*

In every person's brain, Eve knew, there was the thinky part—the part that calculates trajectories and understands science and sometimes says stop when you're about to make a terrible choice. That was probably the part of his brain that Andrew was operating in right now while he was concentrating on revenge drumming. Beneath that thinky part, there was the raw emotion part—love, sadness . . . rage. Eve had been spending a lot of time with that part of her brain in charge. And deeper than emotion—way, way down in every person—there was animal instinct.

What Eve hadn't realized until this moment was that if someone did something terrible enough . . . like if they call you two-faced in front of the whole school . . . then the animal instinct part might just tell the thinky part to sit down. It takes over, and you basically turn savage.

The cadence went: *BA-duh-duh-BA-duh-duh-BA-duh.*

She untangled her arms from Nina's and Destiny's. Their mouths were moving, but Eve couldn't hear their words. All she could hear was *BA-duh-duh-BA-duh-duh.*

She marched across the gym in a straight line, knocking into anyone who happened to be in her way.

Tica-tica-tica-tica ba-duh-ba-duh-ba-duh-ba-duh BUM.

When she reached the Splatter Painting booth, Eve

slapped five dollars onto the table, and received two handfuls of slimy, glowing paintballs in return. They felt like giant popping boba. The art teacher manning the booth waved her arm toward a large tarp with a few splatters on it. But Eve wasn't here for preschool craft time. She was here to win a war.

Bum-ba tica bum-ba tica BUM BUM BUM.

Eve strode toward the stage, vaguely aware that the art teacher was shouting after her. She pressed through a few clumps of overhyped, glowing body-slammers and headbangers. When she got within striking distance, she let the first paintball fly. It went *splat* against the front of Andrew's drum, leaving a satisfying green glob. He missed a beat.

A few kids stopped jumping and looked in her direction.

She threw another one. It splattered onto Andrew's black T-shirt. He stopped drumming and yelled, "STOP IT!"

Madison shot them side-eye but drummed on determinedly. Andrew tried to jump back in, but he was slightly off the beat now.

Eve thought about Andrew replacing her and that Madison was his *fresh flavor.* The image of Madison showing up in a snake costume on Halloween hit her all over again. She whipped another paintball with all her strength. A hot-pink paint splatter appeared on Madison's drum. Madison shrieked.

The cadence was falling apart. The drumline's perfectly synchronized rhythm was turning into a bag of marbles dumped down a staircase.

Eve thought about Mateo and Jamal laughing at her humiliating Halloween costume and practically chasing her through the hallways with flatulence. Two more paintballs went flying. Mateo's drum turned pink. She aimed for Jamal's snare drum but hit him in the face. Oops.

Jamal roared a detention-worthy word over what was left of the cadence.

The kids in the crowd murmured and pointed and asked each other what was going on. The kids closest to Eve gaped at her. One said, "You're busted." The art teacher had abandoned her booth and was weaving her way toward Eve. Principal Oosterbeek was advancing from the other side of the gymnasium.

Eve ran.

If she was going to get in trouble, she wanted to make it fully worth it. She sprinted to the side of the stage and took the stairs in two leaps. Once onstage, she shouted, "*I'm* two-faced, Andrew? You think?" She pelted him in the chest with another paintball. "Because you're the one who FORKED MY YARD!"

The crowd went, "*OHHHH!*"

The drumline wasn't even trying to play anymore.

She chucked another paintball, but Andrew ducked to the side. It whizzed past him and hit one of the bass drums. The boy hidden behind the drum let fly a very not-safe-for-school word. The kids on the floor whistled and cheered.

Meanwhile, Andrew yelled, "You egged my house! You played mind games on me!"

Since he didn't have any paintballs, he threw his mallet at her. Eve twisted to deflect it. The mallet bounced off her shoulder and smacked Mateo in the head before clattering to the stage floor. With a sound of rage, Mateo threw both of his drumsticks. One hit Eve in the side and one flew into the crowd. Several retaliatory glow sticks came back at them.

"Instead of breaking up with me like a *normal person*," Eve growled, stepping closer and hitting him with another glowing glob, "you dressed me up in FIG LEAVES and invited your *other girlfriend* to come to Halloween in a SNAKE costume!"

Someone in the crowd went, "Daaaaaaaang." Lots of people booed. More glow sticks rained on them.

Principal Oosterbeek commanded, "That's enough!"

Mr. Handen, the band director, rushed in from backstage, sputtering, "What . . . what . . ."

But Madison's response was the loudest. "Don't bring me into your drama! I'm not part of this! I DON'T LIKE ANDREW!"

She stormed off the stage, knocking Eve out of the way with her quads and almost ramming into Principal Oosterbeek. He had to take a few undignified hops to avoid falling off the stage. Meanwhile, Eve regained her balance less than an arm's length from Andrew. She took the opportunity to smash her last two paintballs into his hair. The general noise from the crowd distilled into chants of "Fight! Fight! Fight!"

Andrew made a primal noise, reached over his drums to grab the back of her head, and scrubbed the top of his hair all over Eve's face. She shrieked and pulled away, only to slam into the principal, who put his hands firmly on both her shoulders and said, "Let's go."

Eve spat, "You're a horrible boyfriend, Andrew. And a garbage friend."

There were cheers and boos from the gym floor.

"Look who's talking! You literally read a book about how to be the worst girlfriend ever!" Andrew shot back, as Mr. Handen reached him. Andrew swung his elbows, making it impossible for Handen to get a hold of him.

"You don't know anything!" Eve yelled over the noise of chanting and cheering. "I tried— I wanted to be with you, and *you replaced me*." Eve dug her heels in and fought against Oosterbeek's firm hold, determined to get the last word in.

"You *tried*? To what? Make me love you so you could

break me?" Andrew shouted back, as Handen got hold of his drum harness. "Well, it worked!"

Eve felt like she'd been hit with something much more lethal than a paintball. She said, "What?" but the word was swallowed up in the noise from the unruly mob.

The last thing she heard was, "I hate you, Eve! You made me hate you!" Andrew stumbled backward as Mr. Handen pulled him into the wings.

From somewhere in the crowd, a paintball made a graceful arc before splatting on the stage amidst shrieks of laughter. Principal Oosterbeek gave a stern "HEY!"

A shower of paintballs followed. He barked, "SETTLE DOWN!" Then he turned to the art teacher, who was standing offstage wringing her hands helplessly, and said, "Who's watching the booth?"

She clapped her hands over her mouth.

The answer was: no one. No one was watching it. Kids were jostling each other to grab free ammunition from the giant buckets. Paintballs were flying in every direction. Balloons were popping. Kids were screaming. The "Fight" chant was still going. People were using glow sticks as lightsabers and baseball bats and javelins. A group had tipped over the table at the Splatter Painting booth and was using it as a garrison. Another group had found the leftover buckets of neon paint and weaponized their contents. Eve spotted

Nina, dripping orange and furious, chasing Brendan with a shoe.

It was glow-in-the-dark pandemonium.

Eve didn't resist as the principal marched her offstage. She didn't react when a paintball hit her in the face. She felt like the oxygen had been sucked out of the atmosphere. Because Andrew really had loved her. And now he hated her. And it was all her own fault.

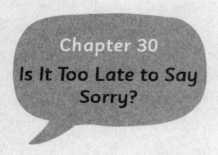

Chapter 30
Is It Too Late to Say Sorry?

The school office was overcrowded. Glow Night had been shut down and most kids had been sent home. But about twenty of them—the worst offenders—had been taken into custody.

Andrew sat sweating, shoulder to shoulder between Jamal, whose knee was bouncing a mile a minute, and a very rigid Madison. They were pressed into the small room with Nina, Brendan, half the boys' basketball team, Destiny, Ramirez, a few of the artsy kids, and of course, Eve. Everyone was various shades of neon, and the drying paint had hardened their clothes and hair into all kinds of strange formations. The office smelled like a mash-up of the locker room after PE and a kindergarten classroom.

Every few minutes, Principal Oosterbeek would call one of them into his office. They'd be in there for a while, and then an adult would arrive to pick them up. Several kids were texting while they waited for their turn—maybe getting their side of the story in with their grown-up before the official phone call.

Andrew thought that seemed like a decent idea, but he didn't want to give Eve the satisfaction of seeing that he cared. Besides, his phone was covered in a rubbery orange film at the moment.

Jamal had his phone out, though, and was texting furiously. Every few seconds he made a noise of frustration or irritation. Andrew nudged him. "You okay?"

"Bruh," Jamal said, his voice gruff. "Reese just broke up with me again."

"What? Why?" Andrew was confused. Hadn't they been holding hands *yesterday*?

Jamal shrugged. "Whatever. I'm probably about to get grounded forever anyway."

Right—because they had broken about a million rules, ruined a school event, destroyed the gym, and gotten paint on practically every piece of percussion equipment the school owned. If Jamal, who had barely done anything, was in deep trouble, Andrew couldn't even imagine what kind of punishment he himself would get.

Andrew had never been in trouble before. He'd never gotten a hall ticket, a detention, a bad grade. . . . It wasn't that he tried to be a Goody Two-Shoes. For him it would just take a lot more energy to break rules than to follow them. So this was a new experience for him. So far, he'd give it a zero out of ten—would not recommend.

This initial phase of punishment was a painful mix of boredom, public shaming, and anticipation of being murdered by his parents. Andrew figured it was worse for him than anybody else here, because they all blamed him (and hopefully Eve) for getting them into this mess. So on top of everything else, he was absorbing their side-eye and muttered accusations.

What if I just said sorry? Andrew wondered. He pictured himself standing up and saying, *I'm really sorry, everyone, but as you saw, it was all Eve's fault.* He already knew how that would end. Restarting the fight right outside the principal's office was probably not a smart next move.

Madison broke some of the tension by turning to Nina and saying, "What are you in for?"

"Oh, me? I dumped a bucket of paint on Brendan, which he a hundred percent deserved. No regrets."

A very green Brendan scowled, and Nina responded with a rude gesture.

Nina turned her attention back to Madison. "Why are you in trouble?"

Madison shrugged. "Shoving Ostridge Beak out of my way, maybe? I don't know. I'm not a part of any of this."

Nina gasped. "Um, so you and Andrew *aren't*—?"

"NO!" Madison huffed. "I'm not interested in any boys—*AT ALL*."

"Do you like girls?"

"NO."

"Sorry if it's not my business," Nina plowed on, "but are you aro? Or ace? It's cool if you are."

Madison looked at the ceiling before leveling a no-nonsense look around the room. "Yeah, it's seriously not anyone's business. But whatever. How about this—I'm thirteen. Can I just be allowed to not be anything yet? I don't want to date any of you *children*. And I don't want to decide what or who I am yet. Okay?"

"That's more than okay," Eve said quietly. "That's . . . awesome."

Madison gave her a scathing look. "*You* don't get to have an opinion. *You* got paint on my drums . . . and accused me of some messed up bullshoot . . . in front of the whole school."

"Sorry," Eve said, looking at her lap. She looked the sorriest Andrew had ever seen her. It made him wish she had said it to him.

Madison blew out an exasperated breath. "To be honest, Eve, I was kind of hoping we could be friends."

Eve's head popped up. "With me? Why?"

Madison shrugged. "You seem cool . . . sometimes."

"So do you." Eve smiled through the film of pink and green that Andrew had smeared on her face earlier.

Andrew shifted in his seat. All of his clothes were suddenly too tight, and he was itchy all over. He tried to tell himself that he was itching because the paint was drying. But it had been dry for a while now. The truth was, it was wishing that was making him squirm—wishing he could be as fearlessly honest as Madison. Wishing that Eve would smile at *him* and call *him* cool. Wishing it was that easy to turn an enemy into a friend.

Eve's words bounced around his head like Ping-Pong balls. *I wanted to be with you. I wanted to be with you. I wanted to be with you.*

In the heat of battle, he'd been too mad to really care what she said. But now all he could think about was that it could have turned out different. At some point, Eve had wanted to be with him, and he had screwed it up. Was it at the dance? Or before that? Or that night at his house? When did it all go wrong?

A basketball player and a middle-aged woman emerged from the principal's office and threaded their way past the obstacle course of legs and feet to the exit. They were very somber. Mr. Oosterbeek appeared and pointed to Ramirez. "Mr. Ramirez, you're next."

Ramirez, looking terrified, shuffled into the office, and the door closed behind him.

Nina turned her attention to Andrew. "Wait. So if you and Madison aren't . . . anything, what was the deal with Halloween?"

Honestly, it was hard to take Nina seriously because she was completely neon orange. Plus, Andrew did not want to talk about it in front of a bunch of people. But there was a small part of him that was glad for the chance to clear his name. He said to no one in particular, "It wasn't my fault." His voice cracked, forcing him to clear his throat and start over. "I mean . . . I did the Eve and the apple part. But the snake costume was just Madison."

Eve put her hand over her face.

Madison backhanded the side of his head. "You freaking noob." She addressed the group. "For the record, it was a *coincidence*. Nobody warned me I was in a minefield."

Ramirez's dad entered the crowded office looking stern. Andrew sank lower in his chair, hoping his friend's father wouldn't recognize him. A few kids helpfully pointed toward Principal Oosterbeek's office door, and Mr. Ramirez disappeared inside. The kids were silent for a tense minute or two, and then father and son reappeared. Ramirez looked miserable, like he was marching to his doom.

Andrew scrunched his face and crossed his eyes. That

made Ramirez stuff his fist in his mouth to stifle a laugh.

Someone else thought it was funny, too.

Eve turned away quickly, but not before Andrew caught a glimpse of her "I'm trying not to laugh" face. The itchy wishing feeling got so bad that it was almost impossible to stay in his chair.

"What's going on in here?" Andrew's mom said as she walked through the office door with Mrs. McNeil.

Andrew groaned, dread replacing all other feelings.

"Mom?!" Eve jumped up and threw her arms around her mother. "You're home?! How did you know to come?" She pulled away and bit her lip. "Are you mad?"

"Mostly confused," Mrs. McNeil said, looking around. "Why is everyone covered in paint?"

"We just came to pick you guys up," Andrew's mom said, "and they told us you were in here. What happened?"

Andrew was hot all over. He looked anywhere but at his mom's face. All the kids were really interested in their phones or shoes or cracks in the wall.

"Mrs. Ozdemir, Mrs. McNeil," Principal Oosterbeek said from his doorway. "Since you're here, why don't you come on in. Andrew and Eve, join us."

As soon as the four of them were packed into the principal's office, he said wearily, "Okay, kids, go ahead and explain to your mothers what you did. Andrew, why don't you go first."

236

There was a big lump of gooey shame in Andrew's throat that made his voice crack about five times as he said, "We got in a fight and Glow Night got messed up."

"Who's 'we'?" his mom asked.

"Me and Eve. And then kind of everybody."

"What? Why? What do you mean by a fight?"

Thankfully, Eve took over so Andrew didn't have to try to explain it. "I was mad at Andrew, so I threw paintballs at the drumline while they were performing."

"And?" Mr. Oosterbeek prompted.

"And called names and, I don't know, there was some screaming and hitting and throwing other stuff. Everyone kind of freaked out, but it was me who started it."

Andrew couldn't believe it. Why would she take the fall for this?

He found his voice. "Actually, it was mostly my fault because of some stuff I did before, and then I said the cadence Two-Faced was about Eve. So that's why she paint-balled me."

"Yeah," Eve agreed, "but I basically deserved it. I mean, you had reasons." She gestured vaguely to her shirt, the words "ANDY O is a total player" barely legible under multiple paint splotches.

"So did you," Andrew admitted. He almost added, *When did you want to be with me? What did I do?* But there were two moms and a principal between them, so he shut his mouth.

The moms shared a look. Then Mrs. McNeil took a deep breath. "I should explain, Mr. Oosterbeek, that Eve has been under a lot of stress at home. Her father and I have been in a rough patch, and it's been . . . difficult. I haven't even been at the house for a couple of weeks. I feel I'm to blame for her acting out like this."

Andrew's heart felt like it was cracking in half. All this time, she'd been dealing with that on her own . . . while he was forking her yard and plotting revenge schemes. Is that what she "didn't need to explain" the night she came over? If only she had talked to him. If only he had known. But then again, he hadn't asked.

He tried to catch her attention, but she wouldn't look at him. Her gaze stayed fixed on her knees. And he wasn't imagining the tears in her eyes. He felt like the worst friend in history.

Principal Oosterbeek didn't notice or didn't care that Andrew was in crisis. He said, "Thank you, Mrs. McNeil. But that doesn't excuse Eve's and Andrew's behavior. We take both fighting and vandalism very seriously at this school. It would be within policy for me to begin expulsion proceedings."

All four of them gasped. Eve turned white. Andrew felt like he was going to throw up.

"But," Principal Oosterbeek continued, "since Andrew has been a model student until now, and Eve's teachers also confirm that—apart from some trouble concentrating in class—this behavior is out of character for her, I am willing to downgrade the consequences to a two-day in-school suspension, during which you will clean the gym, stage, and percussion equipment." He gave them a look that made Andrew squirm, before adding, "With toothbrushes."

"That seems more than fair," Andrew's mom agreed.

Andrew swallowed and nodded.

Eve murmured, "Yes, sir."

"And now," Eve's mom said, "I think the first thing that needs a scrub down is these two. If we're finished, Mr. Oosterbeek?"

He said to report to the office to start their suspensions first thing Monday morning, and then they were free to go. In somber silence, the two moms hustled them out of the office, down the big hallway, and to the parking lot. Andrew knew he should feel terrible. His parents would for sure quadruple his punishment once they got home. He was now going into high school with a suspension on his record. He'd probably be a social pariah after getting into a fight in front of the whole school and ruining Glow Night for everyone. And there was a good chance he'd be playing a triangle in band for the rest of the year. Mr. Handen wouldn't give him any good parts after tonight.

But Andrew couldn't quite bring himself to care about any of that. Mostly he was thinking about Eve—wondering if she was okay, itching to talk to her without three grown-ups presiding over their trial . . . and really, *really* hoping it wasn't too late to say sorry.

Chapter 31
Crash Landing

Gravity felt crushing as Eve walked from the car to the front door. Every step was weighed down by the thousand-pound truth she was carrying. *You made me love you. . . . You made me hate you.* Andrew could have loved her back. But she broke him. She'd thought she was saving her family, but that was broken too. It was all for nothing.

She was also worried about what would happen next. At the very least she was about to get grounded. Plus there was no way to hide what was really going on with her and Andrew now, and Mom would be so upset. Eve was relieved that her mom was back, but she wasn't naïve enough to think that Mom being home meant everything was fine now. Would this be a fighting night or a silent treatment night?

What if her mom only came back to pack her stuff so she could leave for good?

The more Eve thought about it, the heavier her legs felt.

When they walked in, Dad was pacing the living room. He stopped, gaped for a second, and said, "What happened to you?"

No *Welcome home, Jo*. No acknowledgment of her mom at all. Any hope Eve had of a reconciliation crumbled.

Mom said, "Eve, go get cleaned up and then come back down. I'll fill Dad in."

Eve trudged up the stairs to her room, peeled off her paint-stiff clothes, and got into the shower. The warm water ran off her in rivulets of hot pink, fluorescent yellow, and neon green. She watched until it ran clear, dreading more by the minute what she would face downstairs. Eventually, as the water started to go cold, she scrubbed her hair and face before getting out. After drying off, she went to her drawer and stared into it for too long. She was facing a real wardrobe dilemma.

She knew that, at minimum, she was going to have to fess up to her parents about what happened tonight and the months of questionable activities that led up to the fight. It called for her cleanest, neatest, prettiest outfit. Something that said, *I'm your precious darling girl. . . . You can't stay mad.*

But confessing was the absolute least of her worries. There was a real possibility they were going to give her The

Speech tonight—the one that all kids of divorce get from their parents. Everybody knows it goes, *It's not your fault. It's not about you. We don't love each other anymore, but we will never stop loving you.* And then they rip your family and your heart and your life in two.

To face something like that, Eve figured, you needed your favorite cozy clothes. But on the other hand, there was a good chance that whatever she wore tonight would be tainted forever. So she should choose something that she'd be fine with never wearing again.

After a long mental debate, she put on her oldest pajama pants. They were super comfy but completely threadbare. In some places the thin spots had disintegrated into holes with frayed edges. The pants were becoming less fabric and more empty space, one thread at a time.

She found two fuzzy socks that were both missing their mate. And then, after another moment of hesitation, she dug out Andrew's hoodie from a pile on the floor. She pulled it over her damp hair and down past her butt. It smelled slightly musty—less like freshly showered ready-for-school Andrew and more like just-woke-up-on-Saturday Andrew. It also wasn't warm from his body heat like the first time she'd put it on. Worst of all, wearing it was a reminder that she had broken someone beautiful and lost him forever. But it still felt like wearing a ghost of a hug.

It wasn't exactly body armor, but it was the best she could do.

When she got downstairs, Mom and Dad were sitting on the couch, a full cushion between them. They weren't talking. Mom gestured for her to sit in the armchair across from them. Eve sat. She wrapped her arms—encased in oversized hoodie sleeves—around herself and wished it were over.

Mom took a deep breath, waited, and eventually said, "I don't even know where to start."

Eve studied the unraveling hole in the fabric at her knee. *Things unravel,* she told herself, *and life goes on.*

Her pajama pants. Her family. Her friendship with Andrew. Everything unraveled.

Dad cleared his throat. "What happened with Andrew? Why'd you get into the fight?"

Eve tried to sum it up. "Things have basically been getting worse and worse since we went to that dance. I guess I finally just snapped."

Mom put her hand on her heart. "Why didn't you tell me? I thought you guys . . ." She trailed off.

Eve confessed, "I know you want me and Andrew to be a couple, that you've wanted us to get married since we were tiny kids. And you were so happy when we got together."

"See? Too much pressure," Dad muttered.

"Not helping, David. At all," Mom quietly warned

before turning her attention back to Eve. "Hon, I don't care if you date Andrew or not. I mean, I *love* Andrew. And I love you. But who you want to date and eventually marry—that's for you to decide."

Mom knew all the right words, but Eve wasn't buying it. She said, "What about 'oh, young love' and 'you guys are so cute together' and all that stuff?"

Mom held her palms out. "I was being supportive. You *told* me you liked him. Why would you fake that?"

"I thought that by dating Andrew I could make you happy and then you . . ." She gestured vaguely between her parents. "Maybe you guys would . . . be okay."

"Oh, honey! You don't have to try to fix us." Mom said, mirroring Eve's gesture. "This isn't about you."

It's not your fault. It's not about you. The Speech was beginning, and it felt even grosser than Eve had thought it would. She blinked back tears. Tried to numb herself to the rest. She wished she were little again—that age when everything her parents said felt reasonable and true. Then maybe she could just accept The Speech without sustaining too much damage. But she couldn't. And, really, why should she have to? Why should she let her parents off the hook with a few canned clichés?

She gritted her teeth. "Did you seriously just say this isn't about me?"

Both her parents blinked at her, looking earnest, clearly thrown off by her reaction.

Eve couldn't sit still anymore. She stood, muscles twitching. "Of course it's about *me*! What you guys do—it affects *me*. It's my family too, not just yours. You can't destroy *my* family and then say it's not about *me*."

Mom's hand went to her mouth.

Dad's voice was the kind of calm that sounded phony. "Evie, we know it affects you. We're sorry. I hope you know that we both love you."

They're actually reading straight from the script, thought Eve bitterly. She filled in the next line for them. "You'll always love me. You just don't love each other anymore."

Mom sobbed once behind her hand. "Oh, baby."

"*I'm not a baby!* I know what's going on. You literally left us!" Eve shouted.

"Just for a couple weeks. I told you! To clear my head," Mom protested. "I'm here now."

"For how long?"

Her parents shared a glance. Dad nodded as if to say, *You do the talking.*

Eve braced for impact.

Mom swallowed. "Eve, I know it's been rough for you. It's been hard on us, too. And it's not going to suddenly be all cupcakes and kitten whiskers. But we're *really trying*. We're going to keep working on it. We're not getting a divorce. We talked a lot while I was staying at Auntie Jen's, and we're going to start seeing a counselor on Tuesday."

"Why?!" Eve demanded. She wanted to accept this as terrific news. She really did. But she couldn't let herself hope. The crash landings hurt too much. "What's the point? Why bother? You obviously can't stand each other."

"I made a vow. *We* made vows," Dad said, "and vows are stronger than feelings."

"What does that even mean?"

Dad leaned toward her, elbows on his knees. "Feelings come and go. They change. But no matter how you feel, you can decide to keep your promises. Your mom and I stood up in front of everyone we know and vowed, 'For better or worse, till death do us part.'"

"So—just because you repeated some ancient words in a church *seventeen years ago*—you're going to stay married to someone you hate and be miserable forever?" Eve couldn't believe she was saying this. It was like she wanted them to get a divorce.

But it was real, and she was so tired of fake.

Mom looked as wretched as Eve felt. Her voice was high and tight. "Not all marriages can last. Sometimes splitting up is the only path back to some kind of health and happiness. But—" She looked at Dad with something like determination and just a hint of musty, threadbare affection. "We're going to fight like anything to keep this family together—to keep our vows to each other and to you. It's been hard, I know. Your dad and I . . . we let a lot of little emotional debts pile up that never got dealt with. And lately, with me going back to work and Dad taking on more at home, there's been some new stressors that brought it all to the surface. But we're working through those things."

Dad laced and unlaced his fingers. "We do still care about each other. We're trying to remember how to show it."

Care was not *love*. It wasn't enough. But it was so much more than she'd let herself hope for. She could feel tears rolling down her cheeks, tumbling off her jaw and onto her neck. She mopped her face with Andrew's hoodie sleeve. "For real?" she croaked.

"For *real*." Mom stood from the couch and put her arms around Eve. A second later, Dad's arms wrapped them both in a hug. Mom murmured, "You don't have to hold this family together, Eve. You can just be a kid, okay?"

Eve cried. Really cried—the ugliest, loudest, howling meltdown of her life. She felt like she had just survived the roughest reentry in the history of spaceflight. Her heat shield was cracked, her parachute was in tatters, and she had barely made it out of a Mach 5 tailspin. But she could breathe the air. She could trust the atmosphere. The ground was solid beneath her for the first time in a very long time.

Chapter 32
Grand Jester

Andrew's parents didn't even let him take a shower before laying into him. He had not been wrong about the amount of trouble he would be in.

He stood in the living room while his mom told his dad what had happened. He stood there until his shoulders ached, while his dad gave him the "this isn't how we raised you" lecture.

"Where is your integrity?" his dad asked. Andrew knew he wasn't supposed to answer that. Dad continued without pausing. "I thought we taught you to respect others. To treat people the way you want to be treated. How are you fourteen years old and still don't know that screaming and throwing things isn't how you get your way? I am so disappointed right now. . . ."

His dad was building momentum. This was going to be a while. Andrew wished he could take a shower. He was stiff and sticky all over because of the dried paint. His clothes felt like they were made of cardboard. One of his eyes tried to glue itself open every time he blinked. He peeled a fluorescent yellow fingerprint off the pad of his thumb.

"Are you listening?" his father demanded.

"Yes, sir."

Reassured that he had Andrew's attention, he handed out his punishments. Andrew stood still, only nodding his acknowledgment of each one.

They would take his phone. He'd get it back after he had written and delivered apology letters to Principal Oosterbeek, the school maintenance person, the art teacher, the PE teacher, and Mr. Handen. For the rest of the month, he was grounded from video games, which would give him plenty of time for the double chores he'd be doing.

"Now you need a shower," Dad said, ending on a deep sigh.

Finally. Andrew turned to go.

"Wait!" Dad held out his hand. "Phone."

Andrew put the paint-smeared phone into his dad's open palm. He figured he deserved all the punishment he was getting, so he couldn't really be mad at them. But the phone was a real loss. All hope of calling or texting Eve was gone. Not that he knew what to say anyway.

As he turned again to go, he felt his dad's arm come around his shoulders and pull him into a hug. His parents always ended punishments with a hug and an "I love you."

This time Dad said, "Andrew, you're a good person. You're growing into a great young man. I hope you know I love you, and I'm glad you're my son."

"I know," Andrew said into his dad's shirt. "I love you too."

"And I love you too," Mom said, cutting in on the hug as Dad backed up to give them space.

Andrew was a little taller than his mom now. He could wrap his arms all the way around her with room to spare. He could probably pick her up if he wanted to. But she was still his mom. She was still the person who brought him his lunch when he forgot it and felt his forehead when he had a cough, and got the grass stains out of his favorite jeans. It didn't make sense that she had seen the mess he was in with Eve and hadn't stepped in to help.

"Mom," Andrew sighed. "Why didn't you tell me about Mrs. McNeil being gone?"

"It wasn't my story to tell. It still isn't. Eve should get to tell you what she wants you to know, from her perspective and in her own way."

Andrew realized that was true. His mom really was the wisest person. He should listen to her more often. They stepped out of the hug, which had gotten almost awkwardly long. Dad was gone. He had walked off at some point, presumably to put Andrew's phone in lockdown.

"Mom, you know how you said I should talk to Eve?"

"Yeah."

"I don't know how."

She gave him a questioning look, and he shoved his hands into his pockets. "I want to talk to her, but so much stuff has happened, and it feels like we aren't even speaking the same language anymore."

Mom caught her bottom lip in her teeth for a moment before asking, "If you *could* speak the same language, what would you say?"

"That I'm sorry. And I miss her."

Mom smiled slightly. "That's a good start."

Andrew tried to scratch his head, but his hair was like a spiky helmet. "But when I try to say anything to her, we end up fighting. Besides, Dad took my phone."

Mom's smile got wider. "Why don't you get in the shower," she said, "and then come back down, and I'll teach you all about the grand gesture."

"The what?"

"The shower!" Mom said, swatting at him. He knew he'd have to comply before he got any more information out of her. Plus, he really did need to get this paint off.

💔 💔 💔

Andrew scrubbed at his wet hair as he crossed the hall from the steamed-up bathroom to his room. He felt so much more human than he had half an hour ago. He was keyed up to find out what his mom had been smiling about and to make a plan for how to get through to Eve.

"Hey, bro," Tom called from his room. "Come here."

Andrew veered toward his brother's bedroom, and stopped in the open doorway. The walls were covered with Brazilian jujitsu participation awards. The floor was covered in dirty laundry. Tom sat on his bed, his phone screen casting a blue light on his face.

"What?" Andrew asked.

"Check this out. You're famous."

Andrew moved closer so he could see the phone screen. It was a video of him and Eve going at each other just a couple of hours ago. At the time, he'd felt so savage. But on video, they just looked like overgrown toddlers having a tantrum with finger paints. He put his face in his hands and groaned.

Tom laughed. "And look at this one."

Andrew looked through his fingers at a slo-mo live photo of a paintball hitting him in the face. It looped every couple of seconds, so he got to see himself get pelted over and over . . . and over. It said #Team_Eve across the top.

Great. An anti-Andrew hashtag. Just what he'd always wanted. He pleaded, "Make it stop."

"Just one more," Tom said, scrolling. "This is hilarious."

The "hilarious" one was a video of him and Eve being dragged to opposite sides of the stage, still screaming at each other. Not his finest moment. In fact, he'd really like to forget this whole day had ever happened. But at least this one said #Team_Andrew.

Tom was oblivious to Andrew's agony. "I can't wait to show these to my friends. They are going to pee themselves laughing."

"Come on, man," Andrew said. "It's embarrassing enough."

"What are you talking about?" Tom said, like Andrew was being ridiculous. "Why would you be embarrassed? Plus, I watched the video like fifty times—she was being a total d-bag. I'm glad you let her have it. You know what? We should booby-trap her front door, so the next time she comes out, she gets ice water dumped on her or paint or something."

For a second, Andrew pictured it. The bucket poised over the doorway, rigged to tip when she opened the door. It would work—he knew exactly when to set the trap. Eve was always the first one out her front door on Sunday mornings, going for her weekend run. She'd open the door, ready to do her pre-run stretches, and find herself doused in Sherwin-Williams Terra-Cotta Sunrise. She'd scream in outrage, only to have paint run into her mouth.

The picture made him sick to his stomach. It made him want to punch whoever did that to Eve. Which would be a problem if it was him.

Andrew loved his brother—he was cool and fun and dated different people every week and had a driver's license, and when he tensed his abs, he almost had a six-pack. Sometimes Andrew wanted to be just like Tom. But at this moment it occurred to Andrew that some of the things that had damaged his relationship with Eve the most had been Tom's ideas—like the Halloween costume and the whole idea of trying to annoy her into breaking up with him.

The problem was that his brother had never really loved anyone. He saw Eve the way he saw all girls—like they came with unlimited free exchanges. To Tom, if things didn't work out with one person, he could find a different one to fill the exact same space in his life. He didn't understand that there was nobody else like Eve. No one that could fit into the Eve-shaped hole in Andrew's heart. That's why Tom thought the solution to everything was for Andrew to do whatever would feel like a quick win or make the most people laugh on social media.

But that's not what Andrew wanted at all. What he wanted was to love Eve. He wanted to be there for her in any way she needed him. He didn't care if he was her friend or her boyfriend, really, as long as he could be the person she talked to when she was worried about her family. The one she knew she didn't have to hide her tears from. The guy she laughed with and slo-mo karate-kicked and ran to when she was excited or delighted or terrified.

Andrew didn't know if there was any way to get what he wanted. All he knew was that he was willing to take all the work, all the pain, and all the blame on himself if that's what would get him back to Eve.

But he couldn't explain that to Tom. His brother would just call him a wuss or something. So all he said was, "I gotta go."

Mom was waiting for him at the kitchen table.

"What's a grand jester?" he demanded impatiently.

"Grand *gesture*," Mom corrected, eyes twinkling. "It's a way of communicating big feelings."

"Will it fix things with me and Eve?"

She shrugged. "No promises. The other person is always fifty percent of the equation. But I like the energy here."

"*Mom*," Andrew moaned, "just tell me what to do."

She spread her hands. "First of all, the gesture has to come from your heart. So no one else can tell you exactly what to do."

Andrew opened his mouth to protest, but she held up her finger and said, "You need to think about how and when you can show Eve how much you care about her in a way that she is most likely to receive it."

Andrew let his head fall onto the table. "Come on, Mom. I'm fourteen. Don't be cryptic."

She laughed. "I'm not trying to be cryptic. Okay, examples . . . Like one of the most famous movie scenes is when John Cusack stood outside this girl's house holding a boom box over his head."

Andrew didn't lift his face off the table, but he turned it just enough that his mom could see him roll his eyes.

"Okay . . . it's like . . . running through the airport before they get on a plane or speeding down the highway to stop their wedding or singing to them in front of the whole school. Stuff like that."

"Are all these from movies?" Andrew asked suspiciously.

Mom looked sheepish. "Yeah."

Andrew sat up. "Mom?! Does anyone do this in real life?!"

"Not often enough." She rested her chin on her hand and looked a little dreamy. "But . . . yes. In real life people do things like write 'Will you marry me?' on a beach with shells or make candy posters to invite someone to prom. Those are grand gestures."

Andrew thought about it for a second before venturing, "So, like texting, but with a creative medium."

"Sure. That's one way to think of it, I guess. Nice use of 'medium' by the way."

Only half listening now, Andrew muttered, "We learned about it in art."

He needed to think.

While he sifted his ideas, he drummed on his legs. Mom, thankfully, didn't interrupt him. When could he deliver a gesture? Where? *Ba duh duh dum.* What medium would make Eve hear him out? What did he need to say? *Ba ba ba duh duh duh ba ba ba dum.*

Suddenly he went still.

"Andrew?" Mom said.

"I have a plan." Andrew thought he sounded kind of cool and tough, like guys in movies. But when he added, "And I *really* hope it works," his voice cracked and ruined the effect.

Eve woke up with her thoughts spiraling. She had cried so much last night that her eyes felt swollen and her throat hurt. But it was good crying. The kind of crying that makes a person feel clean and empty—like all the dread and grief and anger got poured out of her soul and now it was possible to pour something different in. Not inevitable. But possible.

Even though she knew things still might be tough between her parents, she felt like she didn't have to worry about it anymore. Maybe a little, but about a thousand percent less. They were working on keeping their vows, and they had promised to tell her straight out if that ever changed.

She was kind of worried about school stuff. Her two-day in-school suspension would start tomorrow. She really hoped

Ostridge Beak wasn't serious about the toothbrush thing. And that she didn't miss anything important in science class. The real punishment would come from her classmates, though. What she and Andrew had perpetrated at Glow Night was the kind of drama that middle schoolers could get drunk on. She was pretty sure she'd be the center of attention in the worst possible way. All she could hope was that people would get distracted by something else in a week or two.

Eve couldn't resist checking her phone—forty-eight texts. Most of them were screenshots and screen recordings that her friends had helpfully forwarded to her so she'd know who was #Team_Andrew and who was #Team_Eve. It wasn't pretty. And definitely not going away anytime soon.

She groaned into her pillow and pulled the covers over her head. Maybe now was the right time to volunteer for that one-way lifelong Mars mission.

But Eve's mind couldn't dwell too long on Mars or school or social media. It was in orbit around something with inescapable gravity—Andrew. Would he ever speak to her again? Should she text him? Could she make herself go over and grovel?

He definitely knew about her parents now. That was for sure. But why would he even care? He hated her. She'd broken him. Even if she groveled and Andrew forgave her, that didn't mean their friendship could ever course-correct enough to land somewhere good.

It was all too confusing and horrible. Just thinking about it made her feet jiggle and her leg muscles twitch. She yanked back the blankets and launched herself out of bed. She needed to run.

A few minutes later, Eve was on the front porch wearing joggers and Andrew's marching band hoodie. She took a couple of minutes to stretch before starting out. She knew she should keep her pace slow at first while her muscles warmed up. But she really wanted to sprint as fast as she could. She held herself to a fast jog.

She almost missed the chalk. She actually did a double take and then ran backward a few steps to make sure she'd seen it right. It looked like a text bubble drawn on the sidewalk, big enough to fill one whole square.

She jogged in place for a few seconds, glancing around to see if someone was nearby. But it was early, and the street was empty. Only Andrew called her McNugget. Was this his way of breaking the ice?

"Hi?" she said back to the still morning. There was no answer. Of course.

She ran on.

Half a block later, there were two more messages.

> YOU WERE RIGHT

> I WAS ACTING LIKE A JERK

It was obviously from Andrew. But when did he have time to write her sidewalk texts? How did he know she'd see them?

A drum began to sound in the distance, as if in answer to her silent questions. *BUM—tica-tica-tica-tica BUM duh-duh BUM . . .*

Andrew *had* to be the one playing. But it wasn't coming from his house. Did he know she was out here *right now*? Was he playing for her? The only person who could answer all her questions was drumming somewhere close by. But maybe he'd already answered the only question that mattered. He wanted to make up. He wanted to talk.

She kept running, a little bubble of hope bouncing around her rib cage.

Every few squares there was a new message.

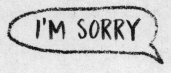

> I'M SORRY

I WISH I COULD ERASE THE PAST TWO MONTHS

I MISS YOU

With every message, the bubble of hope expanded. Eve felt like she might float off the ground. And maybe it was her imagination, but it seemed like the drumming was a little louder. Like she was heading in the right direction. Too quiet for any unseen neighbors to hear, she said, "Where are you?"

A few squares later she ran past:

HEAR THAT DRUMMING? THAT'S ME ☺

Eve laughed. It felt like the sidewalk could hear her and talk back. Andrew was pretty impressive to have pulled this off. She wondered if Tom had helped him and then immediately felt herself tense up at the thought.

IF YOU DON'T WANT TO TALK TO ME THAT'S OKAY

"No!" Eve said a little breathlessly, her heart squeezing. "I do want to!" *Just, please, leave Tom out of it.*

> # IF YOU DO WANT TO TALK TO ME FOLLOW THE SOUND OF THE DRUMS

Eve ran fast, the cold November air whipping her cheeks. She kept scanning the sidewalk for more messages, but as the park came into view and the drumming sounded closer and closer, she started searching for Andrew instead.

She saw him while she was still far off. He was standing near the playground with his quads harnessed on, his sticks a blur. *Bum ba-duh bum ba-duh tica-tica-tica-tica.* Her feet kept time with the cadence.

A little closer, and she could see his eyes locked on her. He watched her approach, unsmiling, without missing a beat. She couldn't get a single clue from his face or his body language about how this was going to go down.

The closer she came to him, the heavier her legs felt. Facing him meant facing up to what she'd done. And if she didn't do it right, she would lose him forever. She had no idea what to say. She hadn't had time to rehearse a speech or buy him a "please forgive me" present or even wash the crust off his sweatshirt sleeves. This was going to go horribly.

About ten feet from him, she came to a stop.

But she couldn't make herself talk. She just stood there looking at him and panting, like a weirdo.

Tica-tica-tica-tica BUM duh-duh BUM BUM BUM.

The cadence came to an end, and Andrew's mallets stilled. The last beats reverberated around the park.

Andrew looked unhappy. Or . . . concerned? His eyebrows pinched together. One dimple popped where his mouth pulled to the side.

"Where'd you get the drums?" Eve asked. It was the least important question, but it was the only thing she could think of to say.

Andrew looked down as if to verify the quads were still there. "Oh, my dad knows Mr. Handen . . . 'cuz they're both teachers and stuff."

That didn't really answer the question, but Eve's brain had already moved on to the next-least important question. "How did you know I'd . . . ?" An arm wave substituted for the words she couldn't find.

Andrew's cold-pink cheeks got a little pinker. He didn't meet her eyes, and he sounded embarrassed. "You always run on Sunday mornings."

Eve looked at her feet, feeling all kinds of awkward but not sure why.

"Sorry if this is weird," Andrew rushed to add. "I just . . . really wanted to . . . to tell you . . . to ask you—"

"Me too," Eve blurted. "We need to talk."

Neither of them said anything for a little while, or even looked at each other. Needing to talk and knowing what to say were totally different things.

Finally, Andrew's voice broke the silence. "Are things really bad with your parents?"

"They're a little better, actually," Eve said, half smiling. "I thought for sure they were getting divorced, but they told me they're starting marriage counseling, so. You know. Maybe they'll figure it out." Eve peeked at him without lifting her head up all the way. "Speaking of which, I might need some emotional support brownies on Tuesday nights for a while. That's counseling night."

"Oh!" Andrew suddenly hefted his drum harness over his head and set it on the ground. He unzipped his backpack, produced a plastic container, and held it out to her. "I made these with my mom last night."

Eve stepped closer to take the container. "Brownies?!"

Andrew smiled shyly.

"My favorite!"

"I know." Andrew scratched his head. "You said brownies make everything better, right?"

Eve opened the container and took a deep breath. She was too nervous to eat right this second, but the smell was enough to make her think she didn't want to join the Mars mission after all. No matter what, Earth was where the brownies were. And then—for no apparent reason and with no warning at all—there were tears in her eyes, too many to blink away. She turned to hide her face, but not fast enough.

"You're crying?" Andrew asked.

"No."

"About the brownies?"

"No," Eve insisted. She wiped her face on her sleeve.

"It's okay," Andrew offered. "I cry all the time."

Eve laughed one *ha*. "I definitely cry more than you."

"No way. I'm like a world champion crier. I never see you cry."

"Shows what you know." Eve smiled and sniffed. "I bawled my head off last night. Snot everywhere."

Andrew chuckled. "Gross, McNeil."

Could they do this? Just slide back into teasing and pretending something like crying was a competitive sport? It felt like so much still needed to be said.

Eve's legs felt tense. She did a quick hamstring stretch.

"You wanna swing?" Andrew indicated the swing set right behind her. Eve suddenly realized that he'd picked this spot just for her. He knew she couldn't stand still for a whole conversation.

They sat in the swings and lapsed into silence again as they both pumped their legs, going higher and higher. The hope bubble in Eve's chest cavity swelled up again. The sidewalk texts, the drumming, the brownies, the swings . . . Andrew had thought of everything. He knew her so well. And he must have spent hours on it. He wasn't Dark Matter Andrew after all. He'd done all this and said he was sorry, when really it was her that had messed everything up.

Eve dragged her feet in the rubber chips, bringing herself to a stop. Beside her, Andrew's swing stilled too. "Um," she said, searching for the right words. "The thing is . . . all the stuff I did to you was terrible, but I didn't mean to break you, and I'm really sorry."

"It's okay."

"It's not. Stop lying."

Andrew went, "Ha." Then he sniffed, and Eve was afraid to look at him because he might be crying. "Just tell me *why*," he pleaded.

Eve could barely force words past the planetoid of shame and regret that had suddenly plunked into her lap. She stammered, "At . . . at first I just asked you to the dance because.

I don't know. Everyone said I should. And it really wasn't a big deal. But then my mom—" Eve got stuck for a second, and then the whole confession poured out of her. "She was excited about us dating, and I started to think that if I could make her happy, she'd stay, and then I thought if you broke up with me, she'd feel sorry for me and *stay*, and by the time I realized that I couldn't make her stay no matter what, I was sure you liked Madison, and I didn't know *what* to do, but you were just being stubborn, and, well, you know how competitive I get."

Andrew was quiet, his swing swaying gently. Eve knew he was letting what she said sink in. She let the silence stretch out, even though she was slowly dying inside. Finally, Andrew said, "So the whole time, you were just using me to get under your mom's skin. You never did want to be with me."

Eve put her face in her hands. When he said it out loud like that, she sounded like an actual monster. She almost said, *Yes, but I'm so sorry.*

But then she thought about the way Andrew had made Mateo Ramirez laugh in the principal's office last night when everything seemed so bleak. She loved that about him. She remembered a hundred times when Andrew had made her laugh like that. Just thinking about him dating someone else had made her so jealous. She still wasn't over the moment when she thought he was going to kiss her. Or the nervous, fluttery feeling when she saw him waiting for her in this same playground, all dressed up for the dance. She'd just about melted onto the floor watching him take the stage at Glow Night. And there was that delicious feeling that Andrew was wrapped around her when she put on his sweatshirt.

The truth was so mixed up that she didn't even know how to say it.

"Andrew," she said cautiously, "I'm going to try to tell you something, and I'm pretty sure it's not going to come out right, and I might have to kill you after."

"Okay?"

"I like you *so much*, and I can't always tell if it's friend-like or . . . something else."

He looked up from his knees then, right into her eyes, and her brain started glitching. She leapt out of the swing and paced. Her thoughts went haywire, but her mouth kept moving.

"You're cool and sweet and funny, and you're my best friend. And I guess I'm trying to say that I . . . I love you. But I'm thirteen. And there are days when that feels like an actual disorder—like my brain and my heart and my body and my *face* are all out to get me. I can't trust myself. I don't understand myself. Half the time I don't even like myself. And the thing is, the thing is—*I don't know.*"

"Eve." Andrew's voice was low. He stood up, clutching the chains of the swing.

She couldn't stop to listen. Couldn't stop pacing. Couldn't stop verbally spamming him. "I can't bear to lose you, Andrew. But I don't blame you for hating me. I'm a mess."

"Eve," he said a little louder, this time capturing her arm on her way past and bringing her to face him. "I love you too. And I'm confused too. Feelings are weird."

He was telling her he understood. That she was okay. Even though she'd spent the past two months pushing him away, he was *still here*. Eve didn't know whether to cry or laugh, so she did both at the same time. It was an ugly hybrid abomination. A cryghff.

She retreated to the slide and sank down on the end of it, sobbing and giggling. When she finally calmed down, she sniffed. "Sorry about your sweatshirt. I just got snot all over it. Again."

"It's okay."

"I'm gonna give it back."

"You don't have to."

"I *really* do."

"Why?"

Eve smiled to herself. "I don't want to explain it. I just want you to wash it and wear it, okay? Then, when you least expect it, I'll take it back. And you aren't allowed to ask questions."

Andrew shoved his hands into his jacket pockets and looked at the ground. "Eve." He dug his toe into the rubber chips like he thought he might find the right words buried there. Then he took a deep breath. "I don't think I can handle the roller coaster again. Where you're nice to me one minute and mad or blowing me off the next, and I never know what you're thinking or which version of you I'm going to get. I just . . . It's too hard."

When Eve was nine, she fell out of the big tree in Andrew's front yard. It literally knocked the wind out of her—she lay there for what felt like hours, unable to pull any air into her lungs, wondering if it was possible to survive this feeling.

She felt the exact same way right now. Like Andrew was pulling away from her and taking all the air with him and she would never be okay. As she sat there trying to remember how to breathe, her dad's words from last night came back to her. So she said them. "Vows are stronger than feelings. That's what my dad told me."

Andrew stared at her, his brows pinching again.

She explained, "Since our feelings are out of control, and we can't really trust them, maybe what we need is a vow."

Andrew said, "Uh." He scratched his head.

Eve stood and held up one hand like she'd seen in the oath of office ceremony. "I, Eve McNeil, vow to never trick you or use you again, Andrew Ozdemir. I vow to use my words even when I'm panicking. And I vow to care more about your feelings than what other people think. As long as I live, so help me God."

They stood looking at each other for so long that Eve started to worry that Andrew thought the vow thing was creepy-weird. She wanted to run. She should probably run. She forced her feet to stay stuck to the ground.

Finally, Andrew said, "Now what?"

"Now you make me a vow," Eve said. "If you want to."

"What do you want me to vow?"

"To never ghost me again. And to never buy me another Halloween costume."

Andrew solemnly put one hand on his heart, but his eyes twinkled. "I, Andrew Ozdemir, being of sound mind and body"—Eve laughed, but Andrew talked over her—"do earnestly and sincerely vow to always text you back, answer your calls, and nod to you at school no matter who's looking and even if it makes a pack of girls giggle."

Eve punched him in the arm.

Andrew stuck the index finger of his other hand into the air, like a statue of a Founding Father or somebody. "And I vow to fully support your freedom of choice and pursuit of happiness each year on October thirty-first, even if you dress up like a planet and spend the whole night explaining to people that you are *not* the blueberry girl from Willy Wonka."

"Hey! My Neptune costume was sick!"

Andrew grinned. "Now do we spit on our hands?"

"Gross. No way." Eve crinkled her nose at the thought. "But we can shake hands to seal the vow."

She offered him her right hand—the same one she'd held up to take her oath. But instead of shaking it, he reached out his left hand and wove his fingers through hers. He'd held her hand like this once before, at the dance. Only this time she didn't want to run away. She wanted to stay forever. She took his other hand, sliding her fingers between his the same way.

They both stared at their intertwined hands like they were witnessing a miracle. Eve's heart raced.

Andrew sighed. "We're only in eighth grade. I don't want to be like Jamal and Reese. Or Nina and Brendan. Or Tom and his weekly girlfriends. You're too important to me to do that."

Andrew's words felt true and heavy and bittersweet. Eve wanted to be Andrew's girlfriend. She wanted them to belong to each other. But she also didn't. She didn't want to risk turning him into her ex-anything. Not ever again. She wanted them both to be kids for a while longer. This felt like a quiz question with no right answer.

She started to pull away from their *very* not-just-friends

hand-holding, but Andrew tightened his grip, not letting her go.

"Eve," he said, "wait. Please stay. Just for a little while. Before we go back to being only friends."

Eve could feel the blood pulsing through her whole body. She could feel the baby hairs on her arms and the back of her neck. She could feel every tiny point of pressure where Andrew's skin was touching hers. It was like she'd only been half-awake her whole life until now. She wanted this feeling to last forever. But she also wasn't ready for it.

"Promise me you won't date Holden," Andrew demanded.

"Huh?"

"Or anybody like him."

"Why?"

"Promise."

Eve was more than happy to say, "I solemnly swear I will *never* date Holden."

"Or anybody—"

"Or anybody like him."

Andrew swayed closer, touching his forehead to hers. "Promise that, even when you don't like yourself, you'll remember that I like you."

That vow was harder to say because she knew it would be harder to keep. "I'll try," she said, not much louder than a whisper. "I promise I'll try. Brownies are probably the best way to jog my memory."

"Right."

Every part of her heart felt tender and fragile. With a burst of self-protection, she blurted, "Promise you'll never take another girl home for brownies. That's our thing. Yours and mine."

Andrew put their intertwined hands over his heart. His jacket was unzipped, and Eve could feel his heart drumming a comforting rhythm. "All brownies shall forever be Eve's brownies," he promised, "or may God have mercy on my soul."

Eve tried to tell him to be serious, but it was hard to talk because she was laughing. And then it was even harder to talk because his arms were so tight around her. It was a totally new kind of hug. Not a rib-crushing competition. No brute force. He wrapped her up and pulled her close, and she melted into him with a sigh of relief. *Change,* Eve thought, *isn't so bad after all. Not everything unravels. Some things evolve.*

Neither of them pulled away for a very long time.

A soccer team showed up and started arranging cones and nets on the open field. A dog barked at them, straining at its leash as its owner dragged it down the sidewalk.

Real life was setting in. They stepped apart.

And then Andrew dropped to one knee, clasped his hands together, and said, "Eve McNeil, will you *please* break up with me?"

Eve crossed her arms defiantly. Dating had been an utter disaster, of course. Things were so much better this way. She could feel the buoyant little hope bubble, the reassuring weight of all their vows, the safety of their long hug. Their friendship had survived a Category 5 emotional hurricane— she knew she could trust it to endure whatever growing up threw at them. And she knew that they both had a lot of growing up to do.

She could imagine how it would be after they broke up. She'd say, *Race you home.* Andrew would accuse her of cheating because his quads weighed a ton, so she'd offer to walk backward to make it fair. They'd eat all the brownies before they got home. He'd call her McNugget. Even though so much had changed—and she knew they'd keep changing— what she and Andrew had together was solid and reliable. As strong as a vow. As sweet as a brownie.

She told herself it wasn't a loss to break up with him. Not really.

But Eve couldn't admit defeat. She couldn't say the words. Instead, she said, "You break up with me first."

Andrew got off his knee, muttering "Stubborn" under his breath. But Eve could see the smile beneath the eye roll.

"Fine," he conceded. "We break up with each other at the exact same time on three."

"Fine," Eve agreed.

"One . . . two . . . three."

"Let's just be friends."

And just like that, they were.

Best. Friends.

Forever.

Acknowledgments

Jessica Smith, this is just as much your book baby as mine. I love co-creating with you! You balance editing genius with mad amounts of encouragement and support. Also, shout-out to Samantha Bouchet, Heather Palisi, Sophia Lee, Elizabeth Littrell, and the whole Aladdin team—you combed through every detail of this book, cleaned up my messes, made it beautiful inside and out, and turned my words into a book. Seriously, you're my heroes. Thank you!

Super Agent Kim Lionetti, thanks for being my publishing sherpa, legalese interpreter, and deal-maker!

Mary, Karen, and Traci—The Charglings—thank you for reading the messy first draft chapters and giving all your writerly insights. I really don't think writing would be much fun without you. Christi, Kerry, and Monica—my moonwallies—thank you for cheering me on and for the late-night read-aloud with white chocolate martinis! Christi, you are doing an amazing job as the president of the G.F. Miller Fan Club!

Matt, every word in this book owes you its life. I wrote while you did grocery runs, cleaned, cooked, and shuttled kids around. I've lost count of the times I heard from the other room, "Mom's writing right now. What do you need?" You are my favorite and the best partner in life I could ever imagine. I <3 U.

Elsa, Annika, and Emory—it's not a hobby. Also, thanks for making me laugh and giving me never-ending inspiration ;-) Ezra, you have no idea how much I loved it when you wanted to talk about *Glimpsed* with me. I hope you think I got this one right! Finally, to all the librarians, you make the world a happier, kinder, more accessible place to live. Thank you.

About the Author

G.F. MILLER absolutely insists on a happy ending. Everything else is negotiable. She is living her Happily Ever After with the love of her life, three kids, two puppies, and some chickens. She cries at random times. She makes faces at herself in the mirror. She believes in the Oxford comma. And she's always here for a dance party. You can visit her at gfmiller.com.

FALL IN LOVE with these swoon-worthy romance novels.